ABOUT THE AUTHOR   RICHARD COOPER

Richard Cooper lives in Staffordshire, England, with his girlfriend Barbra and their ten year old Labrador Bailey. Dead Walk is Richard's first novel.

ISBN: 978-1-84944-091-2

British Library Cataloguing in Publication Data.
A catalogue record for this book is available from the British Library.

Published by UKUnpublished

UKUnpublished
.co.uk

www.ukunpublished.co.uk
info@ukunpublished.co.uk

DEAD WALK

By

Richard Cooper

1

The lay-by was nothing more than a roughly hewn space cut into the muddy grass verge. It was full of loose stone chippings and deep puddles. From the silence of the vast countryside came the faint purr of a car engine. It grew louder as the vehicle approached and seconds later rain-slick tyres were splashing through those puddles as Lewis Crocker brought his MG Rover to a halt.

He exhaled wearily, tiredly, but kept the engine ticking over.

Crocker was dressed smartly; black trousers and shoes, crisp green shirt. His tie matched it evenly and blended in like a chameleon. He surveyed the lush greenness of the Shropshire countryside that hemmed him in from all sides with gritty, tired eyes. It was hard to believe, really, that this tiny place was actually a village. All Crocker had seen to give it away was a small white sign on the mud verge just behind his car.

Welcome to Oak Ridge.

Dwellings around the village seemed to be few and far between. From his current vantage point Crocker was able to see one run-down farmhouse surrounded by cluttered machinery and old, leaning barns. The rear field was heavily overgrown with rapeseed, while the front field had two healthy cows grazing in it. To his left stood a row of Victorian houses, five of them in all, with matching bay windows and steep orange rooftops. He surmised that further up the main road he would come across the coaching inn, The Woodman's Rest, where he had a single room booked. He removed a packet of cigarettes from his trouser pocket and placed one between his lips. Before he lit up, he wondered how the inn survived in such a small community. He supposed that, during summer months like this, Shropshire was plagued with tourists. Driving the thought from his mind, he used a cheap plastic lighter to ignite the tip of his cigarette, drew on it deeply, and eased the car away from the verge.

His guess was correct. The inn was indeed a ten second drive up the main road, standing proud behind a tall wrought iron fence. The building was blockish and squat with lots of sash windows and mullioned glass, while thick green ivy crawled across the structure like a wild infection. Its roof was a huge thatched affair, with several dormer windows cut into it like eyes peering out from beneath long hair. Crocker swung his MG in through the open gate and eased the car into an empty space near the inn's back door.

He wound down the window and finished off his cigarette, eyes taking in details of his new surroundings. The rear of the inn looked slightly scruffy and unloved. Two overflowing wheelie bins stood near the back door, lids raised up as bulging bin bags shoved against them. Crocker watched three flies darting to and fro around the bins, obviously attracted by the bad smell.

A little further along, he could see three tall windows. The one towards the end must have been open, because he could see part of a white lace curtain flapping in the warm breeze. He jabbed his cigarette out in the car's ashtray, and sat behind the wheel for a moment, collecting his thoughts before clambering out and stretching his limbs. The silence of Oak Ridge seemed to drop from a great height and drape itself across his shoulders. Where was everybody? He hadn't seen a single person, or car for that matter, upon entering the village.

He glanced all around him before heading off towards the front of the inn. Once there a firmly closed door greeted him. Beside it, drilled in to the wall, was an old-fashioned ships bell. It was made from highly polished brass with a rope dangling from the clapper. Crocker reached out and chimed the bell loudly, three times. He pulled his lips tight in what could have been a smile and waited for a reply. This was the part of his job he hated the most. The waiting. The long hours sat in silent rooms drinking flask after flask of tepid coffee. It never seemed worth it; until something happened. Not that he expected much from this case, however. The director at the Institute of Psychical Research & Development had offered him this investigation only yesterday, explaining how he thought Crocker would be the ideal candidate for the job. Well, Crocker couldn't help feeling a little bit cheated. Ideal candidate? Bullshit. Nobody else wanted to do it and Crocker was last on the list. Again.

Taking in a deep breath, he clanged the ships bell with gusto, cringing as the loud metallic noise echoed off through the silent village. Enough to wake the dead, he mused glumly.

Being 'last on the list' meant he got all the poor assignments. Like this one, here in the village of Oak Ridge, although the case he'd been given had proved to be interesting reading. He'd stopped up most of last night flicking through the thirty-page report his superior had given to him. He'd come across these supposed cases of voodoo before, but never in England. Also, it struck him as rather strange – no, not strange, more unprofessional – of the Institute to send him out on such an unlikely case; a case that, in his humble opinion, did not warrant an investigation.

Annoyed now, Crocker grabbed the handle and gave the front door a big shove. It opened smoothly and swung right back on its nicely oiled hinges. The psychic detective paused for a moment before stepping over the coaching inn's threshold. He found himself in a well furnished lobby; a lobby that was utterly deserted.

"Hello?" he called, walking over to the reception desk where somebody should have been sitting. Crocker hesitated, frowning. "Hello!"

There was a computer on the desktop, along with a mug of coffee and a half eaten iced bun. There was a telephone too, and Crocker eyed it for a second, tempted to ring his boss and tell him what an out-and-out arse-hole he was.

With a grunted laugh, Crocker moved through the lobby and headed towards another closed door with frosted glass panels, ignoring a second door on his right which had a sign saying BAR AREA in the centre. The glass-panelled door obviously led to the main staircase and upper levels of the inn. He opened it, stepped through and flicked his eyes up, down and all around. Indeed, the staircase stood before him, carpeted in a thick green pile. Sunlight lanced in through the high windows and gave the stairwell a feeling of inner warmth. "Hello! Anybody home?" he shouted. "Mrs. Hatton?"

His boss had informed him that the inn was owned and run by Mrs. Grace Hatton, thirty-six, separated, two children. How his boss knew so much about her Crocker had no idea.

Set into the wall on his right hand side was yet another door. It was open slightly and he assumed that Mrs. Hatton and the kids lived in the room beyond.

Only a deep, unwelcoming silence replied to his demands.

Thoughts of voodoo cults flashed through his mind. Last night he'd read about how Oak Ridge had attracted the attention of a man known as Billy Bracket, a firm believer in voodoo and the black arts. Apparently, Mr. Bracket had five or six followers who all lived in a tiny basement flat somewhere in Oak Ridge. People claimed to have heard chanting and singing late at night, smelt incense burning at all hours, and noticed that the basement flat windows were painted black. That wasn't all. Reports had leaked out from somebody – who had *not* given their name – that Mr. William 'Billy' Bracket was a fully-fledged *bokor;* a sorcerer of voodoo.

How this information had come about puzzled Crocker. Furthermore, he was torn between the best and most efficient way to investigate such claims. Maybe he could arrange an interview with Billy Bracket; one-to-one and with a camcorder to capture any evidence of this guy's supposed 'magical abilities;' although the possibility of capturing something like that to film amused Crocker on a subconscious level.

Shaking his head, the paranormal investigator wandered towards the door on his right, eager to get settled in one of the rooms and take a long, hot shower. He gave the door a light push with his fingertips and sent it swinging inward.

A noise from somewhere inside the room caused him to stop dead in his tracks, his heart thumping wildly. The sound was muffled but audible, and Crocker's highly tuned ears detected it as a terrified whimpering. He licked his lips and poked his head around the frame.

The room was big, a sitting room and kitchen combined, with three windows running the length of one wall. They each offered a view of the driveway and small garden where flowers swayed in the breeze. Up above him, thick timber beams ran the length of the ceiling, giving the room a warm, cosy feel.

A windowpane towards the rear of the room was smashed.

Frowning a little deeper, Crocker moved forwards. He noticed that all of the broken shards of glass were inside; strewn across the blue carpet. Whoever or whatever shattered that window had done so from the outside. He watched the lace net curtain flap and billow as the warm summer wind blew through.

"Uh, hello, Mrs. Hatton?" he called. "Anybody?"

More whimpering.

Crocker whipped around on his heels and searched the room with wide eyes.

"Who's there? Is that you, Mrs. Hatton?"

A sudden thump caused him to flinch and turn his attention towards a broom closet. Crocker did not move for a long time. He stared at the white painted door, unable to blink. This was a feeling he knew from old: the sensation of not being alone.

Silently, Crocker edged forwards, heading for the broom closet door. He paused right outside it and sucked in a deep breath.

The whimpering continued, broken by tearful sobs.

Crocker reached out and grabbed the knob, twisted it gently, and eased the door open.

The wooden staff cracked against his forehead before he had chance to register anything. With a startled yelp of pain he jumped backwards and stumbled, lost his footing, and thumped down hard on his backside. For long seconds the world became a dim, hazy place. The blow had been well aimed and Crocker would no doubt have a good-sized lump and bruise to prove it.

He blinked, cringed, and tried to stand. He could still hear that agonised whimpering, much louder now, and much closer. "Aw, shit," he moaned, one hand pressed to his pounding head, eyes squeezed shut.

When he opened them again, seconds later, the young girl was standing over him brandishing the wooden staff; which was actually a mop handle, in both hands.

Tears glistened on her ruddy-red cheeks. Her eyes were wet and puffy from crying, and Crocker noticed that she kept hitching her breath, a sign that she had been sobbing for a good while. She was shaking with fury or terror, hard to tell which.

"It's okay!" Crocker said hurriedly. Not relishing another whack. "Take it easy darling, its okay." He put out both hands as if surrendering. "Calm down, its okay, I'm not going to hurt you!"

"A-are you one of t-them?" the girl stammered.

"Just put that down and we'll sort everything out," Crocker replied.

The girl hitched, sniffed, and seemed to relax some. "You have to be very careful around here! They're everywhere now."

"Who are?" Crocker asked, raising himself on one knee. "What's everywhere?"

"Them," she spat, eyes darting left and right. "It might look okay at the moment but . . ." she stopped talking and let out a huge sob. "They've killed everybody."

Crocker's heart did a back flip. "What?"

"The dead won't die though, they get up again! They . . . they . . ."

Crocker leaned forwards and grabbed the girl by her shoulders; he squeezed gently and gave her one rough shake. "Listen to me," he said. "You're not making sense! I can't help you if you don't explain yourself."

Her young green eyes, blood shot and wet, latched on to his. "Stick around and you'll see, mister. They'll come looking for you soon."

Crocker nodded and removed the wooden shaft from the girl's trembling hands.

"I think you better tell me everything, right from the start."

The girl backhanded tears from her cheeks. "No time," she said quickly.

"Why were you hiding in the closet?" Crocker asked.

"I was hiding from him," she said. "I-I think he's killed my muh – muh . . ." she closed her eyes and gritted her teeth. "I think he's killed my Mom!"

Crocker stood up and tried to recollect his spinning thoughts. The girl turned and pointed towards the kitchen. "She's in there, where he left her. If I hadn't have hidden when I did, he would have attacked me as well."

She had spoken the words so flatly and loudly that Crocker began to believe her. Young kids make up stories all the time, but never about things like this. He swallowed and took in a deep breath, attempting to calm his racing heart. Well, there was only one way to prove if she was telling the truth or not.

"I'm going to take a look, okay?"

The girl shrugged, sniffed. "She won't be unconscious for long."

Crocker eyed the girl with deep suspicion. At a guess she was fourteen, maybe fifteen at the most. She was pretty and innocent, with high cheekbones and a flood of golden hair. Crocker moved away, slowly, heading for the kitchenette. As he drew nearer he noticed pots and pans scattered across the floor. A broken mug, spilt liquid – probably tea judging by the colour of it, and then. . .

Splashes of blood dotted the lino, coming from a place just out of Crocker's field of vision, behind the units. He took another step into the kitchenette and spotted a human hand. The flesh on it looked silky white.

"Oh, my God," he whispered. The hand was attached to an arm, which in turn was fastened to the sprawled body of a woman wearing jeans and a black top. She was face down in a splatter of her own bright red blood.

Crocker felt his body go rigid. He went cold, he went hot, and then cold again.

"Ambu . . ." he stopped talking and burped wetly. "Ambulance," he managed to choke.

"Don't you think I haven't tried? My mobile is out of service!"

Crocker was gazing raptly at the injury to the woman's neck. It was ragged and crude. Crocker put one foot out, as if to walk towards her prone body, but his shoe slipped in spilt liquid and he grasped at the unit top for support. He leaned back against the unit and breathed deeply.

The body of Grace Hatton filled his vision.

"What happened to her?"

"Look, its not safe here. We better get moving before he comes back!" the girl insisted, her eyes avoiding the gore splashed kitchen floor.

"Before who comes back? Who the hell did this?" snapped Crocker.

"You wouldn't believe me."

"I think you better tell me anyway!" the investigator roared. "We've got to phone the police! We've got to phone an ambulance . . ."

"You can try," the girl replied, picking up the wooden mop handle. "But it won't work."

"What are you talking about," Crocker whispered, grabbing his mobile phone from one pocket. He flipped it open and, with trembling fingers, began to dial three nines. He raised it to one ear but got only silence in return.

"Damn it!" he spat, trying again.

Silence.

He glanced at the screen and noticed the reception bar flashing on and off. "This is stupid, we're not that secluded out here," he said, prodding desperately at the buttons for a third and final time. He got nothing for his troubles but deep silence.

"I've tried the main telephone in the lobby, too," the girl told him. "That doesn't work either!"

A huge rush of panic tried to surge through his system, but Crocker forced it back down with gritted teeth. "Why?"

"I don't know – the lines must be cut."

"No. Why did he try to *kill* her? Was it an accident? Self defence, what?"

The girl chuckled bitterly. "In this village, there's no such thing as an *accident.*"

Crocker turned his back on the body. "Then why? And what did you mean by 'she won't be unconscious for long?' I'm finding all of this very hard to take in!"

The young girl stepped towards him and grasped his hand inside hers. Crocker saw all-out fear shining within her tear-swollen eyes. "Listen to me," she pleaded. "It's not safe here anymore. It won't be long before they smell fresh blood and come looking for you. He'll be with them too, and he's the worst!"

"Who's *he?*" Crocker snapped, his temper flaring. Then a much darker thought entered his mind: what if this young, innocent girl had actually murdered her own mother in a blind rage about boyfriends or what clothes she should or should not be wearing? What if now, at this very moment, the girl was eyeing Crocker's throat with bloodlust, trying to decide on the best way to slit it open.

The girl scraped her hair back with trembling fingers. "Billy Bracket," she replied weakly. "He's . . ."

Crocker's heart froze. "What? You've seen Billy Bracket? He did *this?*"

This time it was the girl's turn to look confused. She narrowed her eyes and nodded slowly. "Are you a policeman?" she asked.

"I'm a detective, of sorts," Crocker answered.

The girl nodded again. "People like you don't last long around here."

Crocker ignored the remark and turned back to the girl's mother. He built up his flagging courage and moved towards her, stepping carefully over smears of blood and broken crockery.

Once close enough he squatted down and reached out with one hand. He pressed his index finger to her throat. Grace Hatton's flesh was soft and chilly to the touch. Crocker swallowed hard as his finger sank into her spilt blood.

There was a pulse; slow and melodic, but *there*.

"She's not dead. But she needs help, urgently."

Relief washed across Jillian's face. "He came in through the window as I was watching television. I swear he just ran at the glass and jumped! He smashed right through and came at me." She stopped long enough to wipe her nose. "Anyway, Mom was in the lobby and she must have heard the noise because she came running in here and tried to help."

"This was Billy Bracket, who came in through the window?"

"Yes. He's one of them now. He turned everybody else into one and finally became one himself!" she gave a crooked grin and added. "Just desserts."

"Became one of what exactly?"

"Look, there isn't much time. We have to get moving," the girl replied.

Crocker stood up and brushed his hands together. "The only place we're going is the local police station to get this reported!"

Her laugh was so unexpected that Crocker flinched back. "Police? Are you joking? They're in with Billy Bracket. I think I'm the only one left."

The investigator frowned. "Haven't you got a brother or sister? My boss . . ."

"A brother, Philip. For all I know he's dead. Now can we get moving?"

Crocker opened his mouth to ask yet another question when he heard a noise he did not want to hear. In his line of work Crocker was self-trained in taking shocks and surprises – it went with the territory when investigating 'haunted houses' – yet his brain was attuned to the real world all around him; his reactions highly astute.

Yet the noise had been real – the clumsy sound of something moving – and the fingers curling around his ankle were real too, for he felt them tightening, gripping, *squeezing*.

For long seconds Lewis Crocker did not move or react.
He felt the pressure on his leg increase as the fingers clawed at his ankle, gripping tight enough to hurt.
Crocker was aware of this but was unable to gather his senses. The poor woman was obviously coming around; she would be confused and in tremendous pain, yet there was something about her crushing grip on his leg, something that was not *right*.

Gut reaction kicked in and Crocker pivoted his body as if avoiding some unseen object. The hand tried to keep its grip but Crocker practically fell out of the kitchen, backwards, and his ankle was yanked free of the icy cold fingers.

Grace Hatton suddenly lifted her head from the floor and grunted in fury.

Her face was a mask of bruises and cuts; hair tangled and flat against her forehead. Her eyes were open, yet badly dilated; the whites fogged with blood. She fumbled at the kitchen units as she tried to stand, the wound in her neck gaping open like a bloody, toothless mouth.

The young girl at Crocker's side was screaming hysterically and pulling at his arm, pleading with him to follow her, cursing him, *run, run, run!*

Grace Hatton hauled herself up and grinned. Horrific! Monstrous! Evil. Words failed to describe that insane smile. She wobbled at first, as if finding balance very difficult, and then she lunged out from behind the units.

"Holy shit!" Crocker yelled, although he didn't know it. He watched, paralysed, as Grace Hatton flung herself at him, teeth bared, eyes glaring. She lashed out with both hands, fingers hooked, and Crocker felt her nails scrape painfully at his face, gouging into the flesh on his cheek. He screamed in agony and twisted away, bringing his left hand out to deflect her. Instantly, she swiped it aside and attacked with renewed ferocity, using her fingernails like talons to rip and slash at him. She slammed him backwards with her weight and went for his eyes.

Crocker shot out both hands and seized Grace by the wrists; fingers inches from his face, yet she struggled and pulled like crazy, a guttural snarl rattling way back inside her throat.

Grace's head suddenly lunged forwards and Crocker heard a sharp *snap* as her teeth clashed together.

She missed, this time, but if she tried that again . . .

An explosion of agony flared under his right eye and Grace yanked one hand free and drew her nails down his cheek. Crocker swore out loud and spun the woman around as if to throw her away from him. He drove her hard into the sofa's backrest and tried to force her over it, but she fought back and caught a fist-full of his hair.

"Do something!" Crocker shouted to the young girl. "Quickly!"

Grace thrust his head right the way back so that his Adam's apple protruded, ripping out a bunch of hairs by the roots. He grunted loudly and grabbed her arm, twisting the limb violently; so hard he actually heard something pop.

Grace howled in pain and arched her body, lips peeled back from blood stained teeth, giving her the ghastly appearance of a sneering piranha. She tried to kick at Crocker's legs but he dodged aside and gripped her arm tight. Grace suddenly gave a brutal twist and managed to pull herself free. She went for Crocker like a rabid dog, saliva and mucus drooling over her lips and oozing off her chin. She took one swipe, then two, and then three with hooked fingers, hoping to catch the investigator in the eyes.

The wooden mop handle smashed across Grace's temple and broke clean in half on impact.

She pitched violently across the sitting room carpet, legs and arms flopping.

The girl stood to one side of Crocker, holding the broken stump of mop handle in both trembling hands. She was crying again.

Grace lay on the floor near the windows, motionless.

"I told you she wouldn't be unconscious for long," the girl muttered.

Crocker removed a handkerchief from his trouser pocket and eased the white material to the savage wound beneath his eye. It was bleeding heavily, but at least she hadn't blinded him. He leaned back against the units and took in a deep breath.

"Thank you."

"She wouldn't have stopped until you were dead. That's the way it goes."

Crocker nodded. "Yeah, it sure looked that way." He removed the handkerchief and was amazed to see how much blood had soaked into the fabric.

He moved away from the units and approached Grace Hatton's sprawled body. She lay on one side, one arm crushed beneath her. She didn't appear to be breathing.

The investigator hunkered down along side her and frowned. The wound to her throat was crude and ugly, and Crocker was appalled to see tiny puncture marks along side the injury. She hadn't been stabbed or glassed – as Crocker had first assumed – she had been bitten!

Yet there was something else – not on her neck – but under her chin.

"Can you come over here please," Crocker asked the girl.

"I'd rather not."

"When Billy Bracket attacked your mother, what did he do?"

"Look, I'd rather not talk about it," the girl snapped. "It was sick!"

"I'm trying to establish the facts, I'm trying to help! What did he do to her?"

The girl closed both eyes and bowed her head. "H-he grabbed her; he was so powerful I couldn't stop him. He threw her around; they fought, then . . ." she stopped and sighed. "Then he bit her. He bit her like a vampire."

Crocker nodded. "What else?"

"I don't know – I hid didn't I? I was terrified and I hid in the closet."

For a long time Crocker gazed down at the strange mark under Grace's chin. He was poised and ready to bolt if the woman moved or twitched – which he doubted; she was out cold, or truly dead. Whatever the case, it allowed him to get a better look at the little round mark, no bigger than a pin-prick; swollen and raised.

Crocker glanced over at the young girl. "Please come over here," he said. "I think you ought to see this."

The girl joined him near her mother – and he felt for her he really did – but she had to see this, two witnesses were always better than one.

"Do you see that little mark under her chin, right there?" he pointed to it.

"Yes," she replied, frowning. "What is it?"

Crocker raised one eyebrow and dabbed gently at the throbbing wound on his cheek. "Well, I'm no doctor but . . ." he paused and shook his head.

"But what?"

Crocker stood back up and continued to dab at his cheek. He searched his brains for a rational answer but could dredge nothing up. He put it bluntly.

"That's a hypodermic mark. She's been injected."

2

"What's your name?"

"Jillian Hatton."

Crocker smiled and extended his right hand. "I'm Lewis."

Jillian shook his hand limply and tried to smile back, but she was far too upset.

Crocker nodded his understanding. "Seems as though I've walked into the middle of a horror film."

"Except this is real," Jillian said bluntly.

"We have to try and get help for your mother," said the investigator. "I'll go outside and see if I can get reception on my mobile!"

"But you won't," Jillian insisted. "Nothing works around here. It's him! Billy Bracket! He's caused all of this."

"I can't just take your word for that, Jillian," Crocker explained. "I must try."

"Please yourself."

Crocker hesitated, ready to go outside. He glanced across at Jillian.

"Do you know where Billy Bracket lives? I mean do you know where his basement flat is?" he asked.

Jillian frowned. "You *are* a copper!"

"Do you know?" Crocker persisted, ignoring the statement.

"Yes, I do. He befriended everybody, practically." Jillian spoke with an air of experience. "He would stop and talk to me most days when I was walking home from school. He'd be leaning on the gate on top of the stairs that led down to his flat. He's got a really good smile . . ." Jillian gave a very distant smile herself, as if remembering better times. "Everybody seemed to like him, then – then all of this happened." She lowered her eyes.

Crocker moved past Jillian and headed towards the door. "You better come with me," he said. "I don't like the idea of you being alone."

"What about you? Are you afraid yet?"

Crocker avoided the question and guided Jillian out of the sitting room and into the stairwell. Then, moving carefully, he walked back through the glass-panelled door and into the lobby where silence ruled the roost. He stopped in front of the reception desk and scooped up the telephone receiver; pressing it to his ear. No dial tone hummed back to him.

He quickly jabbed at some of the digits but got nothing in return. With a curse he slammed it back on the cradle.

"Told you, didn't I?" Jillian said bluntly.

Crocker eyed the girl for a moment before pushing open the inn's front door and walking briskly outside. It was getting hot now, the sun high and glaring. The rain clouds from that morning had melted away towards the east.

Crocker looked up and down the main road but saw nobody in either direction.

"There has to be somebody," he snarled, "Somewhere. . ."

Jillian hesitated on the top step near the door. "It's dangerous out here, Lewis. They have an incredible sense of smell! Incredible eyesight too!"

The investigator fumbled out his mobile phone and tried, in vain, to get at least one reception bar to make a call. He grunted words under his breath that Jillian didn't understand. The small phone refused to comply, however, and Crocker snapped it shut and thrust it back inside his pocket. For a moment he stood on the spot, pondering their strange situation. His problem remained finding a working telephone and calling in help for Grace Hatton, despite the fact Jillian had mentioned the name Billy Bracket too many times for comfort. His boss wanted a good result on this investigation – the first of its kind in many, many years around these parts – and Crocker was not keen to disappoint.

Grace Hatton needed help – *urgently* – but the investigation kept nudging its way into Crocker's mind where it flashed like a yellow beacon. He turned and gave Jillian a steady, measured look.

"I'm not a policeman. I've been sent here to investigate claims of black magic and voodoo. I'm after a certain person known as William Bracket – Billy to you. I'm a paranormal investigator with the Institute of Psychical Research and Development."

"Oh," Jillian said, her brow crinkled, confused.

"Look, Jillian, I know you're in shock but I need you to help me. Can you take me to his basement flat?"

Jillian nodded slowly, her arms crossed.

"My Mom . . ." she started.

"We'll get help for your Mom, I promise. Which way do we go, left or right?"

They moved off along the main road, walking side by side. Stands of trees and thick bramble bushes dominated either side, broken here and there by small entrances to big houses that hid behind the green foliage. Crocker glanced left and right as they walked, footsteps tapping on warm stone. Oak Ridge was utterly silent. It disturbed the investigator deeply, for every village or town surrounding this place was alive and flowing with the tide of everyday life. This place, however, was dead.

The road curved round and out of sight. They followed it, moving on past an empty newsagents and equally deserted Post Office, and on towards a large, dark bricked Victorian dwelling on the corner of Cottage Road.

"This is the place. It's an old textile mill, apparently. Gives me the creeps," Jillian said, nodding at the imposing building. Crocker stopped and flicked his eyes across the scarred structure. It rose up in to the blue sky and seemed to intimidate them, as if the building was actually squaring its blocky shoulders like a doorman ready to use his knuckles. Banks of windows ran from top to bottom, some of the panes cracked, others caked in years of filth. If there was a haunted house here in Oak Ridge, this was it.

The entrance doors were closed and battered, and to the left hand side of them Crocker spotted some black iron railings and a closed gate. He crossed the road and walked towards it, slowing when he noticed ten steps leading down into the stale darkness. They looked slippery with rainwater that the day's heat could not dry.

"That's it," Jillian whispered. "Down there."

Crocker gave the iron gate a push and it wobbled open. The hinges screamed dryly, having not known oil in many a year. "Reckon he'll be home?" asked the investigator hopefully.

"I hope not."

"You stay here, okay? I won't be a minute." Crocker began to descend the rough steps, one hand clutching the cold iron railing. As he neared the bottom a weird fishy smell prodded at his nostrils. It reminded him of gas leaking from a broken pipe. Before he knocked on the closed door that now greeted him, he brushed his hands together to remove scabs of rusty metal from his palms. To his right hand side there were two windows. Crocker leaned closer, thinking at first that the rooms beyond the glass were pitch black. Then he remembered the report he'd read.

Black paint.

He lifted one hand and used his thumbnail to scrape lightly at the dusty pane.

Nothing came away, no black flakes crumbled to the floor. They had been painted from the inside. "I bet your landlord's pissed," he muttered; glad to hear the sound of his own voice.

"What did you say?" Jillian called.

"Thinking aloud," he responded, edging closer to the door and bunching his fist to knock. The wood looked very old and mouldy, the varnish peeling away like leprous flesh. Crocker knocked four times. The sound was hollow and flat, lifeless.

He waited, and waited. Minutes passed but nobody came.

"You're wasting your time. Not to mention putting yourself at risk," Jillian said, moving down the steps to join the investigator. "Can't we just get in your car and go, bring back help, anything!"

Crocker mulled this scenario over for a moment, clicking his tongue. It was a good idea, the only one they had in fact. They could even risk moving Grace and putting her in the car with them, yet part of him wanted to get inside this flat! He itched to shoulder open the door and snoop through Billy's belongings.

"I suppose we could drive to the next town, find a police station. Come to think of it, why hasn't anybody else brought in outside help?"

Jillian shrugged. "Perhaps nobody wants to get involved."

Crocker turned back to the door, grasped the dulled over brass handle, and forced it down. The door creaked, but did not open. He tried again, this time adding a little more pressure to the old wood. It cracked this time, loudly, and before he could stop himself, Crocker flew inside the flat as the door shot open.

"What are you doing?" Jillian snapped, her eyes blazing in shock.

"Falling arse over tit, that's what I'm doing," Crocker said, wiping his hands down the front of his shirt. He wrinkled his nose. "Smells in here."

He was standing in what looked like a small kitchen, but with the absence of natural light it was hard to tell. He made out vague lumps and bumps – a cupboard here, a stove there. The flooring beneath his shoes felt sticky and crunched when he moved. The smell that he had commented on was strong and bad. It hung in the dark sour air like poison. It reminded Crocker of festering foodstuffs and stagnant water.

Fumbling out his plastic lighter, he ground the flint with his thumb; sparks flew, before igniting a tapered yellow flame. He held it high and squinted into the gloom.

Thick black shadows lurched and weaved in corners as the flickering light tried to dispel them. This indeed was a kitchen that was strewn with debris and stank of decay. He could see spilt liquids and broken glass, piled pots and pans in the sink, dirty rags draped over chair backs.

Suddenly, the light was snuffed.

"Shit," Crocker hissed; his thumb stinging. He ground the flint again and used the flickering flame to hunt down a light switch. There, near the doorframe that no doubt led through into the hall or living room. The switch itself was smudged with oily fingerprints and felt sticky to the touch. Crocker pressed it and a single naked bulb on the ceiling threw out a dirty yellow hue.

Jillian moved into the kitchen with slow, measured steps. She pulled a face at the smell and looked all around her. "How does he live like this?" she asked.

"Badly, that's how," Crocker replied, "very badly indeed."

He turned to the door behind him, pocketing his lighter. He gingerly turned the cold brass knob and eased the door open a fraction. The room beyond was darker than Death's cape. Crocker pushed the door wider and took a step into the void. He scrambled his fingers across the wall closest to him and found another switch.

Click.

The bulb in here seemed much dimmer than the kitchen. It flickered for a moment, as if unused to being turned on. The room that lay under the poor light was fairly large and cluttered. A long low-legged table ran the length of the rear wall, heaped and crammed with bottles and boxes. To Crocker's left there was an old television set with a cracked screen. The carpet was threadbare and seemed to be stained with oil or black paint from the windows. He sniffed at the air and frowned. Although it smelt musty and dank in here, there was another scent overlapping.

Jillian poked her head around the doorframe. "What if he comes back?" she hissed, "I know Billy remember. He won't take kindly to you breaking into his flat!"

"We didn't break in," Crocker assured her, moving slowly towards the table. "The door wasn't locked, was it? I merely opened it and walked in to see if anybody was home."

"I'm sure *that* would stand up in court!" Jillian remarked bitterly.

Crocker stopped level with the crap-heaped table and squinted his eyes. The bad stench and poor light were beginning to give him a sickly, gurgling stomach and a curious floating sensation in the head. He rebuked himself and dry washed his face.

"What's the matter?" Jillian asked.

"Nothing. Well, nothing apart from that funny smell."

Jillian sniffed at the air and nodded. "Yeah, like herbs you mean?"

"Hmm, I've smelt it before, somewhere."

"Probably in other houses that you've broken into," she answered wryly.

The investigator gave the girl a lop-sided grin and picked up a large clear jar from the table. Inside it, liquid sloshed.

Crocker turned and lifted it up towards the light bulb, frowning.

"What is that?" Jillian asked; her voice dulled by shock.

The report he'd read last night seemed to be corresponding very well to everything Crocker was hearing, finding, and, indeed, seeing. Of course, this little find in the jar didn't prove a thing, but at least Crocker felt he was achieving *something.*

"Bufo marinus," he intoned.

Jillian shot him a puzzled glance.

The creatures floated in liquid the colour of urine. The first reptile hung vertical inside the jar, obviously dead. Wrapped around it, *crushing it* seemed to be some sort of dark snake. It had entwined itself tightly around the bloated toad's belly, but some how the toad had managed to twist the snake's head upside down. The toad's slimy flesh reminded Jillian of something toxic and rank.

"That's so gross," she cringed. "My brother would love it."

"I doubt that. These two critters don't make good pets. That one there," he indicated with an index finger against the jar. "Is a sea snake, and the other feller is a *bufo marinus;* the bouga toad. It secretes highly toxic venom that causes rapid heart failure. The *bokor,* a sorcerer of voodoo, normally buries these two creatures together so that they die of rage, effectively killing each other."

"Disgusting," Jillian said, pulling a face.

"Isn't it just? The bouga toad and sea snake are key elements in voodoo and black magic. The death from this toad would be utterly horrific. As your heart fails you'd probably suffer terrifying hallucinations."

Jillian moved back a step, as if worried about the toad jumping free of the jar and squirting its deadly load at her. "Surely its illegal to have one of those things, isn't it? I mean, how did he get it into the country?"

Crocker shrugged. "For the right kind of money and contacts you can get hold of anything these days, illegal or not." He placed the jar down, very carefully, on the table and pushed it to the back. He glanced to the right and saw more jars, big ones and little ones, all containing various paraphernalia. His heart was thumping wildly, causing his throat to constrict and dry out. He picked up another jar and gripped it tight, not trusting his trembling hands. Inside was a dead spider, its legs curled up; body shrunken. Crocker replaced it and dragged across a plastic tray, which held eight or nine millipedes, all held down by a pin driven through their backs.

"He likes his creepy-crawlies, doesn't he?" Jillian whispered.

"I'm not sure if "like" is the correct word," Crocker replied. "All of this stuff is purely ingredients for his work."

"I don't understand. Is he casting spells or something; like in witchcraft?"

"No, not really. I'm sure people *used* to believe the *bokor* was casting mystical spells, but actually they're not. It's all down to poison. Everything I'm seeing here is telling me that Mr. Bracket is trying to create zombies."

Jillian was silent for a long time. She stood next to Crocker twisting a lank of hair around one finger. "Okay," she said. "Zombies." She didn't believe a word.

Smiling, Crocker explained himself. "It all began in Haiti, the zombie story. Only I'm not talking *Dawn of the Dead* here. I mean real zombies don't burst out of graves screaming "Brains!" through rotting vocal cords. The *bokor* and his follower's administered the poison – containing most of the stuff on this table – to innocent victims. Zombies were slaves to the *bokor*. It's a disgusting practice."

Yet there was something missing, and Crocker could not remember what it was.

"But why here, I don't understand why Billy would do such a thing in a tiny village like this?" Jillian said, rummaging through the junk on the table. "Why not London or Birmingham? Manchester? Cardiff even."

"There's no solid evidence he's doing anything," Crocker told her. "All of this stuff proves nothing."

"It proves he's weird!"

"Well yes, granted, but we can't go running around like headless chickens screaming 'zombie outbreak' at the top of our lungs."

"My Mom sure looked and acted like a zombie. She attacked you!" Jillian insisted.

"Wrong again, that's purely a stereotype. Real zombies don't act like that at all. They're clumsy; they can't talk or swallow their own saliva. Basically, they're drugged up to the eyeballs on this stuff," Crocker said, picking up some dried bark. He sniffed it and recoiled at the strong, musty odour. "Yes, your mother *did* attack me, but she was strong, Jillian! I mean she threw me around like a rag doll."

"Perhaps he does something different then, because I've seen, Lewis! I've seen what's been going on with my own eyes." Jillian said.

Crocker returned the dried bark to its correct place on the cluttered table and sighed hard enough to slump both his shoulders. This wasn't the way investigations went. Okay, sometimes he got an odd one, but this was just totally bizarre. An empty village, a body that came back to life, phones that refuse to work and poisonous toads floating in liquid filled jars. Part of his confused mind suddenly clung to something – the way a shipwreck survivor clings to his or her lifejacket – and presented it to him. It involved the Institute's director, but he quickly nudged it aside. Not now. Think about that situation later when you've had time to dwell on matters.

He shook his head and straightened up, remembering that they were unwelcome visitors in somebody else's home. He hadn't noticed that Jillian had found something else on the table-of-horror. Too busy wrapped up in his own musings to see her frowning and dragging the large glass tank over.

Only when he heard the slight splash of water did he glance down.

For a split second he froze in horror, then adrenaline kicked in through his system and Crocker lunged out and yanked Jillian away from the table. She yelped in shock and gave him a withering look. "That *hurt,"* she growled, rubbing her upper arm.

Crocker swallowed hard, felt his heart whamming his ribs. He took a step backwards and said, "Just move well away from the table, Jillian, and don't touch anything else."

"Why? It's only a fish," she snapped, staring down at the plastic tub where the ugly thing floated in green water.

Crocker shook his head, suddenly feeling queasy. "No, well yes it is, but it's a puffer fish! It's worse than the bouga toad. My God, how the hell has he got hold of this stuff?"

"Poisonous?" Jillian asked.

"Deadly. The *bokor* extracts a tiny dosage of *tetrodotoxin* from it. He adds it to the poison, along with all the other substances. The effects are terrible!"

Jillian paled and moved away as instructed. "I want to go now."

"You read my mind," the investigator replied, taking hold of Jillian's shoulders. He turned and guided her from the dimly lit room, glancing back just once at the table and its horrific horde. *I'll be back to check you out again,* he thought. *I ought to bring the police and forensics too, see what they think.*

Crocker and Jillian left the flat and each breathed a sigh of relief.

3

They turned off the lights, closed the front door – firmly – and hurried up the stone steps, thankful of the clean fresh air and warm sunshine. Jillian followed Crocker through the gate, turned, grabbed it, and swung it shut.

Scream – clang!

Without pausing they re-crossed the main road, which was still empty of traffic and people, and walked swiftly back in the direction of the inn. Crocker did not glance back at the dark building on the corner of Cottage Road. If a place could be described as soiled and defiant, then Crocker had found it. The atmosphere in there was wrong – volatile – as if the walls had swallowed the past and could re-play it at random. Of course – psychic echo – he'd come across it before, but that place was stronger, much more powerful. It was true what some mediums said: Bad houses attract bad people!

Crocker shook out a cigarette and lit up, drawing deep.

"Can I have one of those, please?" Jillian asked mildly.

"How old are you?"

"Fifteen – sixteen next week."

Crocker felt his throat dry out his heart rate quicken. "It's a filthy habit, you know," he said, hoping she had not noticed his glowing cheeks.

"Yeah, well, with everything that's happened to me today I think I deserve one!"

Blowing out a stream of smoke, Crocker stopped and handed his pack over. She was right. The poor girl was going through the worst day of her life. Jillian removed one and placed it between her lips. The investigator lit it for her.

"We'll drive to the next town," he said. "Get some help for your mother and inform the police. Then I'll come back here and see what I can find out about Billy Bracket."

"Can I stay with you?" Jillian pleaded.

"No, I'm sorry. Besides which you'd find it extremely boring."

Jillian took a quick drag on the cigarette and sucked hot smoke deep into her lungs. "I don't find it boring at all. I find it *fascinating!*"

They carried on walking, eyes always on the move, hunting for other signs of life, but the village refused to spill forth its dark secrets. Crocker finished his cigarette and pitched the butt. They arrived back at the inn and strode through the open gate and up towards the car park where Crocker's vehicle waited.

As they wandered up the drive, Crocker abruptly stopped, and Jillian crashed into his back, knocking the half smoked cigarette from her fingers. He stood there rigid, eyes wide-open, mouth slightly agape. A mixture of rage and fear flooded his system as he gazed at his car, heart thumping faster by the second.

"What's the matter? Are you . . ." Jillian's voice trailed away as she laid eyes upon the sight before her. "Oh, shit!" she gasped.

Somebody had put the tyres through a meat grinder. Leastways, that's what it looked like. All four had burst under a savage attack, reducing them to useless flaps of black rubber. The Rover sat pathetically on its rims, leaning slightly to the right. The front and rear windscreens had been smashed into jagged cracks and spider-web blurs, the side windows obliterated.

The paint work and body had received a beating too, for the doors and wings were scratched deeply and badly dented, paint gouged away by something blunt and heavy so that bright silver metal gleamed in the sun. Yet it was not so much the damage that caused Crocker's skin to run with goose bumps, it was the writing.

In foot long lettering across the passenger side door and rear panels, in crude capitals and blood red paint:

WHITE TRASH

Crocker read the words over and over, couldn't take his eyes from them. Confusion, anger and fear bubbled in his stomach and knotted it tight. He approached the car slowly, as if worried it would lunge at him screaming:

Look at me, Lewis! Just look at me. I'm ruined! Destroyed. You're supposed to be my owner! How could you?

Yet the car remained silent and battered, like some obscure work of art.

Nothing short of a sledgehammer had been used on the body panels, caving them inwards with enough strength to crack the paint and split the steel.

WHITE TRASH.

Crocker found that his eyes would not stray far from those words. They entered his brain and danced like jesters.

Finding it difficult to form the words, he croaked out, "This is insane."

Jillian was already backing away down the drive, eyes flitting left to right. "Lewis," she called, "Follow me, quickly!"

Crocker turned and glanced in her direction. "What?" he snapped.

Jillian pointed dead ahead, her finger jabbed at some thick green bushes and trees that surrounded the inn. She swallowed hard before saying, "We're being watched Lewis! Look, for crying out loud, *look!*"

The investigator spun around and glared at the bushes.

His stomach cramped painfully and his mouth dropped open.

She was right.

Only it wasn't just one person in those bushes.

There was at least five.

4

Two years earlier Lewis Crocker made a big mistake.
It happened at a party thrown by the Institute's director –
Linden Pascal – Doctor of psychology & parapsychology.
Crocker didn't like him. He was a hard-faced snob of French
descent with too much money and zero respect for his
employees.

The party was for all members of the Institute at one of
London's finest hotels. The crystal drinking glasses, the smart
evening wear and piano music served as an irritant, and
Crocker hated it out-right. He enjoyed noisy pubs with loud
rock music roaring from a jukebox. He longed for raucous
laughter and crude jokes, the clink and clatter of pint glasses;
a working-class atmosphere. Yet here he was, standing in a
plush dining hall holding a glass of chilled white wine and
talking quietly to his work colleagues. He kept pulling at his
tie and shifting from foot to foot, itchy and totally
uncomfortable.

Then, across the large crowded hall, he saw her.

She was wearing a tight black dress which clung to every
contour of her hourglass body. Her legs were long and
slender and shiny brown. Yet it was her hair that caused his
throat to constrict. It floated around her pale face and draped
seductively down her back. Beneath the soft lighting it
appeared to be strawberry blond and Crocker had the
powerful urge to rake his fingers through it, to feel the
softness and smell its clean scent. He couldn't take his eyes
from her and talked robotically to the people around him.

Who was she?

What was her name?

So many questions . . . so easy to have them answered. All he had to do was walk over there in his shiny black shoes and smile at her, start a conversation. Yet his legs refused to move at first; they felt rooted to the spot. Like being a teenager all over again. Finally, however, Crocker *did* find the courage to move. He made his excuses and strolled casually in her direction, hoping against hope that her boyfriend – if she had one – did not suddenly appear at her side.

No boyfriend came. She carried on chatting to three other women, laughing at something one of them had said.

He sucked in a deep breath and went for it.

He smiled and introduced himself. They chatted for a long time about everything but ghosts. Her name, she said, was Lucy, although later on he found out this was a lie. Yet the evening continued; more wine and a finger-buffet were consumed and their conversation turned to relationships. She wasn't seeing anybody at the moment and was starting to get very bored on her own. Crocker had been surprised at this; surely her beauty could attract any man she wanted?

The only time she vanished that evening – to powder her nose she said – was during Linden's long and tiresome speech. The posh moron stood on a chair with his stupid up-thrust nose and thanked everybody for their help and hard work over the last few months. He drivelled on about how psychic research was quickly developing into much larger fields; how more and more factors were being discovered all the time, blah . . . blah . . . blah.

Crocker hadn't listened to rest. He'd waited eagerly for Lucy to return.

She did, and they arranged to meet up after the party – and book a room in the hotel.

Richard Cooper

Lucy became extremely agitated before the party ended, insisting that they should both leave at once and not speak to anybody else – including Linden Pascal. A little confused about this strange behaviour, Crocker agreed. Linden was his boss, yes, but were they friends? Certainly not.

While the good-byes and handshakes were in full flow, Crocker and Lucy slipped from the dining hall and hurried into the reception, giggling like a couple of horny kids. It all happened so fast after that. The double room was booked and up they went.

They made love twice, the second time better than the first as they grew to know each other's body. He kissed her up and down and tasted every part of her, the night passed and neither of them noticed.

The mistake he'd made became apparent the next morning as they awoke to a thunderous pounding on the door. Crocker had jumped up from the bed and ripped the door open – only to find a furious Linden Pascal glaring at him from the corridor.

The left hook from Linden's fist caught Crocker in the nose and broke it, sending him flying backwards over the bed. He'd tried to stand, but Linden charged at him and drove a booted foot into Crocker's ribcage. *Snap.* Two of them cracked.

What followed was utter chaos. Crocker had laid on the floor groaning in agony while Linden stood over him, shouting and spitting insults. Lucy – who was not Lucy after all – begged her father to stop hurting him, but Linden was wrapped up in a blanket of fury and had already called the police.

Her father? The police?

Lucy turned out to be Deborah Pascal, Linden's fifteen-year-old daughter.

*

Crocker gave his head a quick shake – perhaps hoping he could dislodge those dirty memories and send them flying. Yet they remained, always taunting, always *there.*

They seemed to return at the worst possible moments too – like now.

The figures in the bushes were creeping stealthy from cover, shoulders hunched like goblins. They spread out to block off any chance of escape, moving swiftly along the perimeters of the inn's driveway and garden, the sound of their rough and ragged breathing enough to raise Crocker's hackles.

"Run!" he shouted to Jillian, his head jerking left and right, trying to keep track of the scurrying human forms. Two of them dashed past on either side and skidded behind him, grinning like lunatics.

Crocker turned to face them and felt the blood in his veins ice over. They were dressed in civilian clothing; obviously members of Billy Bracket's cult, but they were covered in filth and unable to control bodily functions. A constant tide of saliva drooled over their crazy-smiling lips and dripped to the ground. The warm stench drifting from each figure suggested voided bowels. They stood in front of Crocker and panted like dogs, pitiful yet deadly.

The investigator glanced back in the direction of his car – *is there a chance it would start? Yes, probably, but would it move? No chance.*

Besides, three more hunched, gibbering figures stood blocking the car doors like a pack of starving wolves. One of them suddenly roared at the top of his voice – a big hefty man with arms thicker than tree trunks; a rusty blade clutched in one meaty, blood-stained, hand – and lunged at Crocker as if propelled from behind.

He slammed into the investigator like a bulldozer, driving him backwards. He seized Crocker around the throat with one hand and squeezed, his other flew up into the air, brandishing the hooked blade. It came streaking down and, at the last possible moment, Crocker managed to block the deadly blow by grabbing his wrist. They struggled; spun around, and crashed hard into the battered car. The big man forced Crocker back over the bonnet and added more pressure to his stabbing-arm. The investigator couldn't hold him back! Felt his hand slipping away from the man's hairy wrist. The sharp tip of the blade inching closer and closer to his bulging right eye.

An ear-splitting roar interrupted everything.

A stick of dynamite exploded inside the big man's head. One half of his face simply blasted apart and showered Crocker with hot lumps of brain matter, skull fragments and blood. The strangling hand left his throat at once as the body was hurled lifelessly to one side; crashing hard to the ground. The blade clattered at its side. Reeling in horror and coughing uncontrollably, Crocker managed to choke out, "What the hell?"

He stared down at the twitching body with perplexity, heart slamming. His face was painted red and grey, gore dripping from his chin.

"What the *hell?*" he cried again.

5

"No time to explain," a voice suddenly called, "Just follow me and run like hell!"

Crocker tore his gaze away and turned in the direction of the voice.

He saw a young chap of about twenty-five standing at the foot of the driveway, clutching a huge double-barrelled shotgun to his shoulder, aiming it left and right, one of its muzzles belching smoke.

"For Christ's sake mate, move your arse!" he shouted.

The other hunched figures were rapidly backing away, grunting and snarling, tripping over each other to escape the shotgun's power.

Wiping blood from his face, Crocker turned and stumbled down the driveway. His stomach kept contracting and he knew he would vomit. Once close enough, the young chap grabbed Crocker's arm and began to pull him roughly across the road, the shotgun lowered now. "Come on, run! Work those legs."

"Jillian . . ." Crocker said, "Where's . . ."

"She's with me. She's safe. Come on!"

Together they dashed across the main road and hurried onto the pavement. Without slowing, the young man practically dragged Crocker through a hole in the hedgerow and onto a large and overgrown field.

Everything took on a deeply subdued, sleepy context as they ran through yellow rapeseed, the stalks whispering against their jeans. Crocker's ears were still ringing from the noise of the shotgun. He felt shock creeping through his system. Once or twice his feet stumbled on the moist, furrowed ground beneath the crops.

"Up here," the young chap shouted, pointing in the direction of a looming farmhouse. The very one he'd seen on entering this mad village. Crocker risked a quick glance back over one shoulder and then wished he hadn't.

Three of the 'zombies' were chasing them across the field. They were closing in fast, knees pumping like pistons, faces contorted in fury. Even through his terror, Crocker knew this was not right. If Billy Bracket *was* creating zombies then he was adding something extra to his toxin, something that caused these people to react with such violence.

The young chap veered off to the right and Crocker went on his tail, both of them darting across a large, untidy backyard to the old farmhouse. They scurried up the side of a barn, its green paint flaking away, and arrived at the backdoor to the main building. The man with the shotgun twisted the handle, shoved the door open and jumped inside, allowing Crocker to do the same. Once it was slammed shut and quickly locked, both the investigator and his saviour slumped against the wall, panting and sweating, heads lowered.

"Wh . . . what's going . . . on?" Crocker gasped, sucking in huge gulps of air, even though his neck was throbbing after being strangled.

The young chap suddenly lunged towards the kitchen window and raised the shotgun back to his shoulder, its heavy wooden stock pushed against the muscle.

"Christ knows. Yesterday everything was normal, and now . . ." he stopped talking and sighed heavily. "Christ knows," he said again, quieter this time.

Crocker straightened up and glanced around the kitchen. It was big and well furnished, very clean yet slightly old fashioned. He was standing on red quarry tiles that were sunken and cracked. The cupboards and units were very 1980s but all hung level and straight.

"Lewis!"

Crocker snapped his head to the left and saw Jillian standing in the doorway to the room. He smiled with relief.

"Where did all that blood come from?" she asked, walking over to his side. "Are you okay?"

"Never better," he lied. "Where the hell did you go?"

"You told me to run, so I did. Then I saw John and he told me to get to the farmhouse. I'm sorry . . ."

"No, no it's okay!" Crocker said, alarmed that she should think it was her duty to stop and help him. He stroked her face gently. "I'm just glad you're safe."

"The trouble isn't over yet, my friends," said the young chap – John – from his position near the open window. "They've given up for now, but not for long. You better help me barricade the doors." He lowered the shotgun and broke it. Crocker watched the spent casing from the shot he'd fired clatter to the floor. "They'll attack front and back. We can use tables and chairs, anything to hinder them a little."

"I'm Lewis Crocker," said Crocker, his hands and knees still trembling madly.

"John Yates. Introductions over. Let's make this place safe."

Yates was short but extremely well built. He wore an old green jacket despite the heat, muddied blue jeans and brown engineer's boots. His face was oval and rugged, with pink cheeks and a strong jaw; a good-looking man with farming blood in his veins.

He fumbled inside his jacket pocket and produced another red cartridge for the shotgun, which he thumbed into place and snapped the weapon shut.

"Okay," he said efficiently. He propped the shotgun up against the kitchen wall and brushed his hands together. "The backdoor first. We'll block it with the table, its oak, very heavy. Pile a few chairs on for good measure."

"Look, can I wash my face first? I'm feeling really sick here. I mean, you just *blew* somebody's head off!" snapped Crocker, battling with his gurgling stomach.

Jillian visibly paled. "You killed someone?" she asked, her voice constricted.

Yates rounded on them both, his face twisted in rage, big veins bulging inside his temples and neck. "That bastard I shot was a murderer! He was a total psycho! He killed my father and my brother this morning . . ." Yates abruptly stopped talking and clamped his mouth shut; closed his eyes. "I couldn't stop him. I heard the commotion in the backfield where they were working. My gun was in here and I knew I wouldn't have time to get it. The fucker used that blade to . . ." He turned away and sighed deeply. "Never mind. The point is I sorted him. Plus, Mr Crocker, I saved your life."

"I'm grateful, really," Crocker replied, taking in long, even breaths to stop him from vomiting. "I just want to wash his brains off my face, that's all."

With another big sigh, Yates nodded. "Help yourself. Soap's in the dish on the draining board." He then turned his back and began to drag the solid oak table, single-handedly, across the kitchen floor towards the backdoor, its sturdy legs scraping loudly on quarry tile. He manhandled it around and shoved it into place.

Crocker walked unsteadily over to the sink. He spun the cold tap and began to splash his face with torrents of icy water. He used the slimy bar of soap and scrubbed at his face, wincing in pain as he touched the gash on his cheek. Blood gurgled down the plughole.

Even from behind closed eyes, Crocker could see the man's head popping like a ripe watermelon as the shot removed his brains. He gritted his teeth and gripped each side of the sink. I won't vomit, he told himself. I won't *vomit.*

"Mr Crocker, I'd really appreciate some help," Yates snapped.

Towelling his face dry, Crocker glared icily at the young farmer. "How can you be so cool and emotionless? You've just killed another human being!"

Yates was in the process of dumping two chairs on top of the table. He gave a snort that came across as defiant. "Bollocks man. He was an animal. I've felt more pity for the foxes I've caught in traps. If the situation arose again, I'd do the same."

Crocker shook his head.

"Justice, that's what it was. I simply cut out the middle man and went straight for execution," Yates said; brown eyes fixed firmly on the investigators. He held his hot gaze for a moment before turning back to his work.

"I don't think it's their fault," Crocker pressed. "In my opinion, they've been poisoned."

The farmer spun around angrily and said, "Well, I didn't ask for your fucking opinion, did I?"

"Fair enough. I just thought you might like to know the facts," Crocker replied coolly, taking out his packet of cigarettes.

"What's he going on about?" Yates asked Jillian, as if the investigator were incapable of answering. Crocker went on regardless:

"I take it you know William Bracket? Billy, to his friends."

Yates shrugged. "Think so. Black guy, right?"

"Well . . ." the paranormal detective hesitated, suddenly unsure of himself. How to explain this and not sound stupidly insane?

"Zombies," Jillian blurted. "He's trying to say they were zombies."

Yates chuckled bitterly and shook his head.

"It's true!" Jillian said weakly.

"Sure it is. Come to think of it, Dracula and Frankenstein's monster have started their own taxi firm around the corner."

"Screw you," Jillian snapped; arms folded defiantly across her chest. She hated John Yates and his moronic farming family. Bunch of bigheaded bullies who thought they owned Oak Ridge and everybody in it.

"Anytime sweetheart," Yates leered, "but let's wait until this zombie attack is over, eh?" he shook his head again and left the room.

Jillian flipped him a middle finger behind his back.

Crocker went after him, a smoking cigarette jammed between his teeth. "Look, this is bloody stupid. What's the point of barricading ourselves in here? We need to get out of this village and bring back some help."

Yates huffed. He was already dragging a hefty bookcase across the hallway, meaning to block the front door with it. "Help me with this."

The investigator slammed his palm against the side of the bookcase, stopping its awkward process across the carpet. "No, I can't do that. I'm sorry but you're not cooping Jillian and me up in here."

"Then go. But don't expect me to come along and save your stupid backsides again! If you step outside, you're on your own," he hissed.

"I don't expect you to understand, Mr Yates. I don't fully grasp it myself, but what Jillian said is sort of correct . . . about zombies," Crocker said evenly. "And I'm not talking Hammer Horror here, I'm talking *real* zombies who are normal people dosed up on a deadly cocktail of drugs!"

"You're mad is what you are!" Yates snarled. "Bloody townie."

"Please, listen!" Crocker said gruffly, adding more pressure to the bookcase. "I need you to come with me, back to the body of the man you shot . . ."

"I don't think so!"

" . . . because I need to check something out, something vital."

"Like what?"

"Well, come with me and I'll show you. Look, Mr Yates, this is your farm! This place is your livelihood! Are you going to let Billy Bracket take all of that away from you?"

Yates searched Crocker's eyes, his mouth set in a tight line.

"He's killed my father and my brother. You could say my livelihood is already ruined."

Crocker sighed. "Then come with me for their sakes! Help me sort this out!"

Yates nodded slowly; his jawbone clenched tight, his shoulders stooped.

"All right. I'll come with you. But if I see another of those things, I'll shoot first and ask your permission later!"

6

They left the farmhouse via the front door.

Three people who glanced left and right nervously, bodies tensed and ready to either run or fight; whichever response kicked in first.

John Yates, eldest son of Gordon Yates, now deceased, gripped his shotgun in both strong hands as they hurried across the cluttered front yard. They headed straight for the long metal gate at the foot of the drive and swung it open.

In one of the large side fields, Crocker heard cows mooing as they grazed.

Jillian was holding the investigator's hand so tightly that the blood supply was all but cut off. The day all around them was bright and hot, the air heavy with the scent of manure and rapeseed; a sickly smell that simply *was* the countryside.

Crocker narrowed his eyes against the sunny glare and searched for hunched figures, people with Billy Bracket's poison in their veins. "They could be hiding anywhere," he said to Yates.

"I know," the farmer replied sharply.

"We'll make this quick. All I want to do is check the underside of his chin – if it wasn't blown away that is – just to clarify something in my mind."

They walked stiffly along the footpath, single file, always on the look out.

The inn stood opposite them, its thatched roof thrust up at the shiny blue skies.

As they'd prepared to leave the farmhouse, Crocker had tried to explain to Yates about Billy Bracket – and his horrific basement flat. He told the farmer about the bouga toad and sea snake, about the puffer fish and other grisly beasties that lay on the table-of-horrors. Yates had listened with an air of contempt, sometimes nodding; other times grunting as he opened a drawer in the kitchen and shoved spare shotgun cartridges into his pockets. In the end, Crocker had given up trying to convince him that Billy Bracket had caused this outbreak of real zombies. What was the point? Yates was furious about his father and brother and wanted nothing more than revenge.

All three of them crossed the silent road and stopped at the wrought iron fence, heads turning this way and that like submarines' periscopes. Yates thumbed back the shotgun's twin hammers and gripped the weapon to his thigh.

Crocker peered up the driveway and felt his heart slam like a door. He could see a bulky lump sprawled on the tarmac, a bulky lump with arms and legs. Christ, he really had to do this, didn't he?

"Right," he said, attempting to assert himself for the shock. "You wait here with Jillian. I'll go and check the body."

"What's the point in me waiting down here if you get jumped on up *there?*" Yates whispered, "Unless you can handle the shotgun? Be warned though, she's got one hell of a kick! Probably knock you arse over tea kettle."

"All right, follow me then," Crocker snapped. "Just watch where you're aiming that thing."

Yates lowered the weapon. "After you," he muttered.

Without further hesitation, Crocker moved up the driveway, Yates and Jillian following behind.

They were greeted by the angry buzz of meat flies as they drew closer. Attracted by the scent of death and blooded flesh, they zipped and zapped through the air around the body, sometimes alighting on its mangled head.

Crocker cupped a hand over his mouth and cringed. This was ten times worse than he'd imagined! Fifty times worse if anything. Most of the man's cranium was splashed haphazardly across the tarmac like bright red paint; only paint mixed with lumps of soggy tissue and shattered bone. The smell drifting upwards was offensive.

Jillian turned her back and took in long, even breaths.

Yates and Crocker stared down at the body, the investigator grimacing, the young farmer expressionless. "I got him good, Dad," Yates muttered, "I nailed the bastard for you."

Crocker moved around slightly to the left and squatted down. He flapped three flies away from his face and squinted at the underside of the man's chin.

His heart began to speed up, every hair on his tensed body bristled and his scalp crawled as if suddenly flooded with tiny spiders.

The small puncture mark was there.

A mark caused by nothing more than a hypodermic needle.

"Can you see it?" Crocker asked Yates, "that tiny puncture mark?"

The young farmer hunkered down along side the investigator and frowned hard, creasing his otherwise smooth brow. "Yeah," he replied, head tilted quizzically. "What is that?"

"I assume it's how the toxin is being introduced to the body. How else do you get somebody to ingest something they would normally refuse? Ram the needle under the chin, hit the plunger, and bang! The muscles in the jaw lock up and you have no choice but to swallow," Crocker explained.

"Then come the seizures, the vomiting, and the hallucinations. Basically, the body starts to die – very slowly."

"Is that why they attack?" Jillian asked. "Because of what they hallucinate?"

"It's a theory, isn't it? I just don't understand *why?*" Crocker said.

Yates stood up, glanced behind him, squinted left and right. He saw nobody, but the feeling of being observed was overpowering. "Your car," the farmer muttered, nodding in its direction, "has White Trash written on it for crying out loud! The *why* is racial! This is black against whites."

"Don't b . . ." yet Crocker stopped his sentence at once. He captured that idea and tossed it back and forth inside his brain. It had possibilities. Billy Bracket *is* a black man, and yes, all of the victims in Oak Ridge, so far, have been white.

"He's come up with the perfect plan, old Billy Bracket has. First he befriends everybody in the village, gets them on his side – apart from me, I *never* liked him!"

"You don't like anybody," Jillian hissed.

Yates ignored the statement and continued: "Then he does whatever you say he does, I don't know, cooks up his magic potion or whatever."

"There's nothing magic about it. It's a toxin made from different animal skins and plants," Crocker replied, standing up and brushing his hands together.

"Yeah, yeah, same thing. Anyway, he cooks it up and places it in loads of syringes and waits for the right moment to strike! Perfect. He can stand back and watch the fun as white folk turn against white folk!"

Crocker shook his head, not convinced. "White folks have been killing white folks for years! We don't need Billy Bracket's help."

Yates hefted his mighty shotgun in both hands and his eyes gleamed. "Well, he's picked on the wrong village, hasn't he? Made a big mistake there, he has, fucked up large style. If I see him, he'll get both barrels of this, right?"

"Wrong. We're getting out of here right now. I take it you own a Land Rover?"

Yates narrowed his eyes at Crocker, and straight away the investigator was reminded of a smug tomcat. "We own a Land Rover, yes," Yates said, "but it won't be much good to us. The water pump seized up last week."

"How convenient," Crocker sneered.

"What we need to do is find this Billy Bracket character," Yates snarled. "I've got a bone to pick with him."

"What we need to do," Crocker said, annoyed. "Is get Jillian's mother to a hospital – quickly. Sod Billy, and sod this investigation!"

Yates grabbed Crocker by the shirt collar and yanked him close. "You listen to me you fucking . . ."

"Stop it!" Jillian shrieked, "Just stop it, please!"

The farmer glared at Crocker with eyes like blazing coals. The investigator ripped the hand away from his shirt and stepped back, teeth clenched.

"It should be me you're blaming!" she sobbed. "You want to hit somebody, then hit me, both of you!"

The two men turned in her direction, frowning.

"Jillian?"

"No, Lewis! Listen to me. I . . . I can't carry this on any longer." She stopped, took in a deep shuddering breath. "Don't be angry though, *please.*"

"That depends," Crocker heard himself saying.

Jillian screwed her eyes up tight, big fat tears leaking down both cheeks. She rubbed her face hard with both hands and nodded. "I'll understand if you do get angry, I would too, but please believe me, I wanted *nothing* to do with this!"

Crocker felt the smothering silence of Oak Ridge closing in from every conceivable direction. In many ways he knew what was coming: He'd been suckered in like dust into the belly of a vacuum cleaner. He moved a step closer to the girl and dry swallowed. "Now Jillian, if you're about to tell m . . ."

Yates screamed: "Jesus! Look out!"

Crocker spun on his heels, whirled around like a spinning top, and was just in time to see two shapes dropping amongst them. They landed with heavy thumps; knees bent to take the impact, and lunged at Crocker, Yates and Jillian without pausing. The human brain, by far the best computer ever invented, allowed Crocker mere seconds to work out where they had sprung from. The rear of the inn had been extended at some point, giving it a nice flat roof; a perfect hiding place. Regardless to being hurt or even killed in the process, the two men had leapt from the roof to attack. That could only mean one thing now – that the inn was infested with them!

One of them looked young – twenty-one at the most – his face contorted in fury, eyes wide and staring, saliva drooling thickly over his bottom lip like party string. He was grunting incoherently, muttering words lost beneath mucus and spit. He went straight for Jillian, grabbing her in the crook of his arm around the throat, yanking her backwards. The second, much older, hunched, grey haired and whining like a terrified dog, swung out with the iron bar he was holding, catching the farmer a glancing blow across the face. His head snapped back and he stumbled, dazed and stunned, into Crocker; a gash on his cheek already welling up with blood.

"Help me!" Jillian screamed; the last word choked off as the young lad crushed her windpipe with his arm. Yates bounced back, shook his head to clear it, and swung the wooden stock of his shotgun into the older man's face. It connected with his mouth and teeth smashed under the blow. He howled in agony, dropped the iron bar and staggered back.

"Bloody hell . . . that's old man Vardy! He runs the newsagents!" Yates panted, frightened now, watching the grey haired man – Vardy – reeling in agony.

The younger man twisted his head round and shot Yates a blazing glare of out-right hatred. Whatever he was hallucinating must be twenty times worse than any nightmare Crocker could ever imagine. He clung to Jillian as if she were a rag doll, his fingers sinking into the soft flesh of her neck.

"Help me get him off her, Yates! He's killing her!" Crocker said; his muscles tensed. He moved towards the younger man, unsure what action he was going to take; playing the macho hero wasn't a Lewis Crocker thing.

Yates pushed him aside and threw the shotgun's stock back over one shoulder, meaning to repeat the move he'd done on old man Vardy. Yet the old man with blood now bubbling over his swollen lips moved faster than Crocker thought possible. He snatched the iron bar from the ground, ran at Yates, and swung it hard into the farmer's back, pitching him hard onto the ground. The shotgun flew from his grasp and discharged a mighty roar of heat, smoke and pellets. Crocker instinctively ducked and turned away; eyes squeezed shut, hands raised over his head. The back of his shirt rippled madly, as if yanked at by tiny hands and he smelt burning, *felt* burning, and screamed.

Yet another screech of pain drowned Crocker's voice out, this one high pitched and mewling. It lasted almost five chilling seconds before dwindling away to a clogged gasping.

Crocker found himself turning towards that awful moaning, heart slamming against his rib cage.

Old man Vardy was hunched over; both hands clasped to his groin. A crimson tide was already flowing through his fingers and splattering the ground. Crocker took a step forwards as if to help, knowing that the shotgun had spat most of its deadly load in Vardy's testicles.

"Your back," Yates suddenly bellowed, struggling to his knees, dazed. "Watch your back, Lewis!"

Before Crocker could respond, a freezing cold hand grabbed roughly at his neck and squeezed with alarming strength. He felt long fingernails sink into his flesh, sending bolts of hot agony through his head.

The younger man still clung to Jillian with his free hand; choking her, thumb pushing against her windpipe. He held Crocker too; his drug-fuelled strength seemed to give him the power of ten men. He yanked the investigator backwards and peeled open his saliva drooling mouth, yellowed teeth finding his neck.

The investigator drove one elbow back like a piston and slammed the young lad hard in the stomach. A flood of hot, rancid breath gushed past Crocker's face.

Twisting, he caught a fist-full of the young lad's greasy brown hair and yanked it back. The violent tug sent his head snapping upwards as if he'd spotted something of interest in the sky. Crocker heard tendons crunch inside the neck.

Jillian struggled frantically and managed to free herself, dropping down hard on to her backside, coughing and clutching her throat.

The young lad thrashed his head left and right like a ferocious dog, tearing a clump of hairs out at the roots, leaving them dangling in Crocker's grasp. He then lunged at the investigator with fearsome accuracy, forehead connecting with Crocker's like a sledgehammer.

The blow was startling. A pure white explosion seemed to go off behind his eyes, a nuclear radiance that spread out and enveloped his senses. He felt his body falling like a puppet with its strings snipped; collapsing, folding up. Yet even as he struck the ground he heard Yates and Jillian calling his name, even heard the clatter of the shotgun being reloaded.

Crocker passed out to the thunderous roar of the weapon.

7

" . . . Ooooooiiiisss."

Sounds had no meaning in the pure dark of unconsciousness.

It was rather nice here, anyway. Comforting. Like being back in the womb.

Yet those strange sounds persisted, noises that he recognised, something which gave him identity.

" . . ey, looowwwiiisss!"

He felt the darkness shifting, moving, losing solidity. Colours began to show, bright yellow and smudged pink melting into focus.

He blinked, coughed, and sat bolt upright. Straight away his head swam, white dots flashed before his foggy vision and he groaned in pain.

"Hey, Lewis, rise and shine!"

Crocker leaned back against the soft cushions. The room he lay in was unfamiliar; high ceilings and dark oak panelled walls. The sofa he was sprawled on faced the window, giving him a clear view of fading daylight and trees.

"Here." A glass of water with white froth crackling and foaming on its surface was thrust into his hands. "Two painkillers in there; drink up!"

Crocker squinted at Yates in confusion. "I feel like shit," he croaked, causing Jillian to laugh. She moved closer to him and gently grasped his arm. "You had me really worried, Lewis! I thought you were dead."

He tried to smile reassuringly but it failed big time. "Takes more than a little scuffle to finish off Lewis Crocker," he joked, although what he really felt like doing was curling up and sleeping forever. He took a mouthful of water and painkiller and swallowed gratefully. Fragments of the fight on the inn's driveway began to filter back to his memory. "Oh, no," he said, turning sharply to look at Yates. "I remember now! That old chap – Vardy, he got shot in the . . ." he stopped and grimaced as the gnawing pain inside his skull increased.

"Balls? Yeah, I know. That was an accident. He's dead," Yates said calmly.

Crocker grunted. "What about the other one? The young lad who gave me the Glaswegian kiss? I suppose you removed his testicles as well," he said sarcastically.

Yates strode across his living room and pulled open a cupboard door. He removed a bottle of Haig whisky. He twisted off the cap and slumped down on to a worn armchair. "For your information," he said, taking a long suck on the neck, gulping down whisky. "I fired the shotgun over his head. He turned and ran. Twice in one day, Lewis. Saving your life is becoming a habit."

Crocker drained the glass in his hand, cringing at the powdery taste it left behind.

"How did you get me back here?"

"To coin a phrase: with the greatest of difficulty," Yates replied. "Me and Jillian had to drag you most of the way. You need to diet, Lewis."

Crocker swung his legs to the carpet and leaned forwards, feeling queasy. "Diets can wait. Other matters, however, can't. You agree, Jillian?"

The young girl lowered her eyes and nodded.

"Well?" he pressed. "You started to tell us earlier on, this thing about you 'not wanting anything to do with it.' Remember?"

Yates watched all of this from his armchair, impassive, sucking at the bottle.

"My Mom and your boss," she said wearily. "They've known each other for years, well before she met my Dad. I reckon they had a fling. Anyway, he phones up last week out of the blue and they talk for ages, and I mean *ages*. I tried to listen in, but she told me to go and watch TV and closed the door." Jillian gave a big sigh, as if talking about this was a huge effort. "Okay, this is the part you're not going to like Lewis, and I'm sorry. After the phone call, Mom came into me and said she needed a big, big favour. You've got to remember, Lewis, my Mom and that boss of yours go back a long way, good friends and all that." She met the investigator's eyes evenly. "You slept with an underage girl, didn't you?"

Yates frowned but said nothing. He drank from the bottle. Amber rivulets dribbled from the corner of his mouth and dripped from his unshaven chin.

"Yes," Crocker replied, his mouth parchment dry. He looked down at his hands, fingers laced together. Memories returning, the beating, the broken nose and the police throwing him roughly inside a cell that reeked of bleach. "I had no idea at the time. Okay, that sounds pathetic but it's true. I'm no paedophile. She looked older, much older! I thought she was at least *twenty*." He closed his eyes tight, teeth gritted, guilt surging through his veins. "According to her father – Linden – Deborah Pascal has always been a wild child, but that's no excuse. Apparently, he knew she was there at the party that night! He was even letting her drink alcohol! What kind of a father is he, anyway?"

"Your boss . . ." Jillian began.

"He's an arsehole."

"He wants you dead!" Jillian finished, emphasising the last word.

Crocker snapped his head up too quickly. Pain blossomed. "No, he doesn't like me, but he'd never . . ."

Jillian leaned forwards. "He hates you, Lewis, he wants you dead. You slept with his underage daughter, a girl my age. He – he arranged everything."

Crocker narrowed his eyes. "Everything? You mean he set this whole fucking investigation up?"

Jillian nodded slowly. "Yes, but its all gone wrong! None of this was supposed to happen, none of it! Mom asked me if I'd . . . lure you, try to *tempt* you; make you walk into something you couldn't handle. She said you were evil!"

Crocker felt his anger sparking up like hot blue flames. "Evil?" he growled, "I'm not the Yorkshire Ripper for Christ's sake. I made a mistake. I'm human!"

A heavy silence fell over the room. Nobody spoke for an age.

Then, mildly, Crocker said: "Linden hired Billy Bracket, didn't he?"

"Uh-huh." Jillian said, her cheeks burning rosy pink, eyes watery. "He paid for Billy to come over here, to England." She paused, bottom lip trembling. "It was supposed to be easy. You, as Linden said, would probably get just a little bit *too* nosey, and wind up making a fatal mistake."

"Meaning what?" Crocker asked, his heart throbbing angrily.

"That you'd bite off more than you can chew. I think Linden hoped that you'd stumble across Billy in his flat, and a fight would break out. Billy's not the kind of person to tangle with. He's a big man, plus he's crazy."

Crocker tried to swallow but the simple act was denied him. "A set up," he muttered, "The bastard tried to set me up!"

Yates backhanded whisky from his lips. A vein was bulging near his clenched jaw.

"He killed my dad and brother, Jillian," he said. "Are you saying they died because of *this* prick?" he pointed at Crocker and suddenly threw the bottle of Haig violently to the floor where it smashed. "Is *that really* what you're saying?"

Crocker stood up, almost toppled as his head swam. "Hey, just a minute," he snapped. "I've been taken for a ride too! My own boss is trying to murder me!"

"He won't need to, I'll do it for him," Yates growled, his voice slurred from the whisky. He ran a trembling hand through his hair. "I ought to kill the both of you."

"I'm sorry! What more can I say?" Jillian retorted. "It's Billy! He was supposed to murder Lewis and nobody else. Linden paid him to make it look like an accident, but Billy's insane! I don't think Linden realised just how mad he is."

Yates shoved himself to his feet and teetered dangerously. "I'll show him mad," he spat, turning towards the kitchen. "*I'm* mad! And when I done with you two, I'll show just how mad I am!"

With those words, a brick exploded through the living room window.

The pane of glass burst apart and spewed outwards like razor sharp crystals.
The brick itself, most likely scavenged from the backyard, spun end over end in the glistening shower before striking Yates with a resounding thump on the shoulder.

He grunted in pain and twisted away from the deadly shards.

Before anyone could react, the window opposite smashed with a screeching clatter, sending broken daggers flying through the air. A lump of stone like a clenched fist sailed inches past Crocker and smacked into the wall.

All hell broke loose. More solid objects were suddenly hurled with awesome ferocity at the farmhouse. They heard upstairs windows smash, other things bouncing off the brickwork and more objects were thrown through the already broken windows.

Jillian screamed as a big stone whooshed past her face and gave her a sharp glancing blow to the temple. Crocker grabbed her around the waist and dragged her to safety behind the sofa. He cringed as three more lumps of jagged stone flew inside the living room and struck the furniture. "Yates!" he called, "For crying out loud, get behind here now!"

"Fuck that! I'm going to sort these bastards out!" he growled, shoulders hunched as stones and pieces of broken brick sped past him. A vase standing on the sideboard was reduced to a jigsaw puzzle as a stone hit it dead centre. He stumbled towards the kitchen where his shotgun was propped against the wall. As soon as he entered, the window above the sink smashed and showered him with glass. Tiny pieces sliced at his cheeks and forehead, opening the flesh. He clenched his teeth angrily and snatched the weapon from the floor, hefting it to his waist. "Okay," he shouted, "Let's see what you make of this!" He broke the gun, fumbled out two cartridges, and loaded them.

Without taking aim, unable to see anybody to aim *at,* he thrust the long barrels out of the window and squeezed the triggers. The sudden flash stung his eyes, lit up the dusk, and the roar filled his entire head. Some bramble bushes towards the rear of the yard exploded.

Another huge stone blasted into the window frame, splintering the old wood.

Yates felt a warm trickle of blood running down one side of his face. He briefly touched the gash above his eye and winced. He stepped back, boots crunching on shards of glass. He broke the shotgun open, allowing the spent casings to eject.

With trembling fingers and a whisky-fogged mind, he fumbled two more cartridges from his pockets and loaded them in. He moved back to the smashed window and peered outside, eyes narrowed. The light was fading fast, turning the sky a deep shade of plum. Shadows in the large backyard were total and deep. "Where are you?" he whispered, clutching the shotgun hard enough to turn his knuckles white.

Silence. No more stones or bricks were thrown.

Had he scared them away? Maybe. No, *unlikely.*

A mild breeze hissed through the fields, stirring the rapeseed. He wondered how the cows and pigs were doing, having not been fed or seen to all day. He also thought about his father and brother, lying dead in the field. This only brought on a fresh wave of anger and the need for revenge.

He glanced at the backdoor, where the table and chairs were heaped up against it.

Go outside, he told himself. Hunt 'em down! Finish it right now.

A sudden noise from behind him caused the farmer to twist round on his heels, bringing the shotgun out; fingers tightening on the triggers.

"Hey!" Crocker yelled, hands raised up and trembling. "Calm down, it's me!"

Yates kept the weapon levelled upon the investigator. Both men stared at each other for what felt an impossibly long time. At last, Yates said: "I could squeeze these triggers right now. Blow you through that wall."

Crocker tensed, tried to speak but couldn't form the words.

"All of this mess is because of *you!*" the farmer growled. He moved forwards, those outside momentarily forgotten. "You better answer me some questions, Lewis, because I've got a few loose ends dangling around up here," he jabbed his own temple. "Can you do that for me?"

"Shouldn't we . . ."

"No. I want this mess explaining!"

Crocker closed his eyes and nodded.

Yates stepped right up to the investigator and pushed the warm barrels of the shotgun into his stomach. "First off, zombies," he said. "I can't understand the link between you sleeping with an underage girl and the walking dead."

"They're *not* dead," Crocker replied. "At least, not yet. As for the link, I don't think there is one. My boss, as Jillian indicated, wanted me dead and me only. But Billy has gone crazy, hasn't he, the plan has gone wrong. *Bokors* consider zombification to be the ultimate punishment, given to wrongdoers like me. Once poisoned the victims were buried alive and left for one day, perhaps two before being dug up again. By then most are raving loonies, if not dead from lack of air."

Yates frowned, and then shook his head, not convinced. "Sounds a bit too dramatic to me. Why not just sack you and let you rot in prison?"

"Because that's not Linden's style. He's too sly, too cunning. He wanted revenge and he's waited two years to get it," Crocker replied bitterly.

"And your car was destroyed to make it look like a racial attack?" Yates said.

Crocker let his breath go with a hiss. He was boiling over with rage now.

"Perhaps I should look into karma next. What goes around comes around!"

Yates did open his mouth to reply, but Crocker never got to hear it. Each had made the fundamental error of not watching the windows, backs had been turned and that, like in any war, was the worst mistake to make.

In the living room, Jillian *did* see them and *did* manage to shout: "Lewis! John! They're coming!"

From all directions, closing in fast, men and women turned into monsters by a deadly toxin. They shambled and loped towards the farmhouse, all carrying weapons, all salivating bile and reeking of excrement. They plodded and tripped, stumbled and ran, hating and not knowing why, those who were different from them. Yet the one they feared – their Master of sorts – was not far behind. He guided them; spoke to them in his strange and alien tongue. He was the same as them – yet *not.* In him they smelt true evil and animal cunning. He was quick minded while their brains were slowly dying. He could control them if he wanted; kill them if he liked.

He'd instructed them to attack the farmhouse with the weapons he'd given them and they obeyed.

After all, he was their Master.

Yates flinched at the sound of Jillian's voice. He tore the shotgun barrels away from Crocker's belly and half turned towards the smashed kitchen window. "Shit," he muttered. The farmer took one step in the direction of the window, muscles already tensing, shotgun raising, when the first figure – male, wide eyed, foaming at the mouth with vomit and saliva – appeared like a jack-in-the-box. He gazed into the kitchen at the two men with dilated pupils, the whites heavily blood-shot.

He suddenly lifted one hand and lobbed something yellow and flickering into the kitchen.

In took seconds for both men to realise what it was, and by then it was too late.

The milk bottle hit the quarry tiles and burst.
There was a quick, eye-watering stench of petrol, a flat *whump,* and the fumes ignited.

"Jesus Christ," Crocker yelled, leaping backwards in shock.

Yates jumped out of the way, narrowly avoiding the sudden splash of blazing fuel that dashed itself across the floor. The heat singed his flesh straight away.

"Living room!" Yates shouted, "Stop them!"

How? Crocker wanted to ask, watching the figure at the kitchen window duck out of sight, gone as if never there.

The farmer eyed the crackling flames, heart thumping madly inside his chest. They were threateningly close to the wall now, yellow tongues licking at the green paint, blistering it. He dashed headlong for the sink, meaning to grab a plastic tub off the draining board and fill it with cold water.

Another milk bottle, complete with burning rag stuffed into the neck whooshed in through the empty window frame and struck the wall near Yates's head.

It smashed on impact, throwing out glass and ejaculating blazing petrol.

Yates felt it splatter his shoulder and neck, burning immediately. It flashed down his arm and scorched at the flesh on his face. He screamed in pain and lurched away from the sink, beating at himself; crashing into the table and chairs near the back door.

Crocker dived into the weaving flames, alarmed at how fast they had caught the walls and skirting boards. Already the heat was powerful and eye drying. He reached out and grabbed the farmer by the jacket and hauled the younger man back towards the living room. Somehow, Yates had managed to hold on to the shotgun with one hand, his other red and swollen from beating at the flames.

They tumbled into the living room, coughing as thick grey smoke filled their lungs and churned through the air. Even through this terror Crocker wondered how those drugged up individuals had come up with the idea of Molotov Cocktails.

Not them, somebody else.

He turned and kicked the door shut behind him.

Before any of them could gather their senses, another hunched figure – this one female with wild hair and sunken cheeks – jumped at the living room window, caught the frame with one hand and tossed her petrol bomb in with the other.

Yates was a split-second too late in reacting. He swung the shotgun in her direction and squeezed the triggers. The blast erupted through the room, ear-splittingly loud, and a little off centre. A good portion of the wall and window frame exploded, sending chunks of wood and plaster dust flying. The female zombie howled in agony as some of the shot removed one half of her face. Blood and charred flesh splattered the carpet, along with three of her shattered teeth. Yet the petrol bomb had already landed, breaking against the pine dresser.

As her mewling, twitching body tumbled backwards onto the yard; the fire was eating greedily at the living room furniture. "Put it out!" Yates shouted, fumbling inside his pockets for more cartridges. Two left. Shit!

He was shaking now. With trembling, nervous hands he broke the shotgun open, allowed the spent casings to eject, and slammed in the fresh ones.

Crocker and Jillian were attempting to stamp the flames out, but it was pretty much useless. The carpet was old and dry, perfect kindling.

Behind them, another figure was scrambling in through the opposite window, mindlessly slashing itself open on jagged shards of glass that remained in the frame. It muttered and dribbled angrily, teeth clenched, yellowed bile leaking through the gaps.

It dropped down with a heavy thump and wobbled side to side.

"Look out!" Jillian gasped, jabbing a finger at the newcomer.

It brandished a rusted meat cleaver in one fist, the blade still murderously sharp.

Crocker, still battling with the flames, spun around and saw the figure approaching, the meat cleaver swishing back and forth. He snatched up the first thing that came to hand: a small footstool. Better than nothing, but still rather pathetic.

The figure lunged and took a blundering swipe with the cleaver. The blade whistled as it sliced air. Crocker brought the footstool up just in the nick of time. He heard – and felt – the cleaver bury itself deeply in the underside of the stool, twisting it in his hands.

Yates, knowing his ammo was all but gone, used the shotgun like a club. He rammed the wooden stock hard and fast into the figure's solar plexus. It snorted in pain and flew backwards, eyes rolling in sockets.

Jillian, without realising what she was doing, took three steps away with her back to the broken window. She watched the flames as they bit deeply into the pine dresser. She then glanced at the fight going on between the zombie, Lewis, and John.

Then her swift, wondering gaze fell upon the poker that lay on the hearth. A flare of hope sizzled through her. She could grab it; use it as a weapon!

She put out one foot, meaning to grab the poker and help the two men, but at that very moment somebody grabbed her from behind. Hard, rough skinned fingers squeezed her flesh tightly and pulled her back with frightening strength.

Another hand looped over her shoulder. The index finger rose and pressed itself to her trembling lips. The flesh on that hand was black and the voice that spoke right into her ear was one she knew too well.

"Hush, my darling," it said, so deep and husky. "Baron Samedi says *hush!*"

8

The shotgun's heavy wooden stock crashed into the zombie's nose.

The meat cleaver jumped from its twitching fingers and skittered away across the carpet. The figure slumped, unconscious and bleeding, against the wall.

Panting and sweating heavily, Yates took a step back from the prone figure and sucked in a deep breath. The air was hot and acrid with thick smoke and he started to cough straight away. Crocker picked up the fallen meat cleaver and, eyes watering, turned towards Jillian. His mouth opened and his tongue began to form the words, 'Get out of here,' but they dried up in a split-second and his mouth clamped shut in horror.

Jillian was in the process of being yanked backwards through the window behind her, both arms flailing madly in the smoky air, legs thrashing and kicking.

For a moment he was frozen on the spot. Fire crackled and snapped all around him, singing his flesh, nipping at his legs and thighs like spiteful teeth. Yet he'd seen the tall dark figure pulling Jillian through the window. He'd seen, through smoke and watery vision the black skin and gleaming white eyes.

Billy Bracket.

"He's got her!" Crocker managed to say, seizing Yates by the shoulder. "Billy Bracket! He's taken Jillian!"

"Then she's dead!" Yates retorted, head jerking right to left, watching the fire as it destroyed his home. Too late now!

The telephone wasn't working and his pesky mobile was somewhere upstairs. All they could do was escape the building before it burned them up alive.

"We . . ." the investigator started coughing and couldn't stop. The smoke was so thick and churning. He wanted to scream at Yates, shake him roughly, and demand that they go after Billy and Jillian! She's only fifteen, after all.

Yates pointed to the door on Crocker's left hand side. "Through there. Hurry it up!"

"Please," he croaked, allowing the farmer to push him along.

"Move it."

The fire, as yet, had not spread this far, but that wouldn't be the case for long.

Crocker struggled with the knob and pulled the door open, relieved to see the hallway and front door beyond it. They dashed full-pelt down the hallway, leaving behind the roar of flames and the deadly smoke. Crocker stuffed the meat cleaver down his belt and scrambled with the front door's latch. Behind him, he heard Yates cock the shotgun's hammers. *Clack.*

The only thought that flared within Crocker's mind was to rescue Jillian, even though she had lied to him and deceived him, even though she had taken part in this evil plot to have him killed, he *had* to save her!

He wrenched the door open and threw himself outside; coughing and hacking like the world's worst cigar smoker.

Billy Bracket stood blocking his path. In one powerful hand he gripped Jillian's long hair; in the other he held a slender hypodermic needle.

He was grinning.

9

"Bad boys," Billy Bracket cooed. "Such bad, bad boys!"

He was astonishingly tall and masculine. His chocolate-dark skin was pure and smooth. The dome of his head bore no hairs; likewise his face and chin. Big brown eyes, surrounded by slightly yellowed whites gazed down at Crocker and Yates with rage and – Crocker felt this like the ground beneath his feet – insanity! William 'Billy' Bracket was as mad as a March hare.

He wore an immaculate suit and tie, a designer label, strikingly neat.

Dangling around his tree-trunk neck was a pendant made from different animal bones and feathers. Crocker noticed with disgust that it boasted a severed chicken's foot in the centre, shrivelled and curled. Every time the *bokor* moved that pendant rattled and clicked dryly.

He looped Jillian's golden locks tightly around his paddle-sized hand and pressed her close to his side like a favourite pet.

For long seconds nobody spoke. Behind Crocker and Yates, inside the farmhouse, a smoke alarm was bleeping madly, over and over.

Billy Bracket continued to grin, showing off his crooked teeth. Three of the lower were missing, while somebody – perhaps Billy himself – had whittled his canine teeth down into sharp points. His grin was predatory.

"Bad boys," he said again. His English was good – with a strangely soothing Caribbean drawl. "You stand before Baron Samedi as *bad boys*."

"Let the girl go!" Yates barked, aiming the shotgun at the *bokor's* chest.

"You don't speak to the Baron that way, brother. That be the wrong way of talkin'"

Crocker watched the hypodermic needle in Billy's other hand. It was filled with white fluid. Billy was slowly pushing the air out.

"It's me you want, Billy," Crocker said, even though his heart was thumping hard enough to send him dizzy. He hated needles; the very sight of them tightened his flesh. "Please, let Jillian go and we . . . can talk about this like adults."

"If you address me, brother, you call me Baron. Understand?" Billy said.

Crocker nodded. Oh, Jesus, he thought. He actually believes himself to be Baron Samedi, the God of the Graveyard. Well okay, play this game. Go with it.

"Baron," the investigator said, "May I speak with you alone?"

Billy Bracket continued to grin. He looked more like a crocodile than a human being. He glared down at Crocker with sparkling eyes that radiated intelligence and malice.

Then, from behind a large rusted tractor to Crocker's right, a figure sprang. It jumped effortlessly over the vehicles battered seat and, before Yates could react, it seized the farmer's hair. The zombie used its other hand to whip a knife blade neatly across Yates' throat. He screamed in shock and agony, the shotgun dropping from his grip. Blood welled up and poured from the wound.

Billy Bracket moved with all the grace of a professional dancer, dragging Jillian along with him. He seemed to glide forwards, knocking Crocker out of his path. His left hand, which grasped the hypodermic needle rose swiftly, then dropped like a dagger. It plunged right into Yates' eye, bursting the brown orb in a shower of blood and optical fluid.

The farmer howled like a wounded dog as Billy Bracket thumbed down the plunger and injected his toxin.

At Billy's side, Jillian struggled for all her worth, not caring that a good bunch of hairs got yanked out in the process. She slammed a fist into Billy's kidneys, and the grip on her hair relinquished.

"Silly bitch," Billy Bracket growled, leaving the syringe sticking out of Yates' eye socket like a jabbing finger. For a moment the young farmer stood upright, his mouth gaping, throat slashed grotesquely. Blood poured down his chest, a bright red waterfall. His remaining eye bulged open in realisation, yet the lights were dimming, glazing over as the life-spark ebbed. He dropped backwards, slammed into the door, and fell with a crash into the farmhouse hallway.

Billy Bracket lashed out with one arm and tried to catch hold of the girl, but his large hand missed by a fraction. "You don't *fuck* with the Baron, you bitch! I can hurt you without being *close!*"

Crocker heaved himself up, having been knocked to the ground by Billy's shoulder. He turned and stared down at Yates' convulsing body.

"My God," he breathed. Nausea bubbled in his stomach. Blood, so much *blood*. It was trickling over the doorstep like spilt paint. One of Yates's legs jerked and twitched as if dancing to Death's orchestra. Crocker hadn't liked the farmer, in fact he'd found the man despicable, but his loss was brutal and sudden, uncalled for, barbaric . . . the list could go on forever. The investigator swallowed back an unexpected sob that threatened to rise up his throat and spun round to face the *bokor;* his fists clenched so hard his nails sunk into the soft flesh of his palms.

Jillian crashed into him, arms circling his stomach and crushing his insides. The figure that attacked Yates – the very one that head butted Crocker hours before – scuttled over to Billy Bracket, his Master. He lifted the knife to his mouth and began to lick the blood from the silver blade.

"He was no good," Billy Bracket purred, nodding his head in Yates's direction. "You two, however, *will* be good. My slaves. My children."

"Think again," Crocker retorted. "It ends here Billy. Give yourself up."

Oh, please, that was so lame, his mind screamed.

Billy Bracket laughed explosively. "No brother, why don't you give yourself up to *me?* Be with me, dance with all of us!"

Crocker switched his eyes down, quickly, at the shotgun that lay near his feet.

"I have been told to sort you out, brother," Billy Bracket said, oblivious to Crocker's plan. He dug two fingers inside his jacket pocket and removed a photo. "This is you, bad boy," he grinned, fangs displayed. "I have been told to bring you into the Baron's family!"

"I never liked that photo," said the investigator truthfully. It had been taken four years ago when life was much easier. Linden must have taken it from the Institute's files. The quip seemed to work though, for Billy Bracket glanced down at the picture, taking his eyes from his quarry.

Crocker moved Jillian aside, bent, grabbed the shotgun, and straightened up. Three seconds. Easy. His smile soon vanished as thick black smoke tumbled across his vision, obscuring Billy Bracket and his zombie companion. The farmhouse was quickly turning into huge pyre.

He saw his chance. Grabbing Jillian's hand he turned and began to sprint in the opposite direction. The shotgun was heavy and cumbersome, but he ran hard, Jillian at his side, keeping pace. They dashed headlong across the front yard and aimed for one of the side fields. Behind them, receding, they heard Billy Bracket bellow with furious rage.

"Where will we go?" Jillian asked as they shoved their way through the bramble bush that surrounded the field. The burrs and sharp branches hacked and sliced painfully at arms and legs, but still the pair fought and wriggled through. "Anywhere," Crocker told her, blooded hands clutching the shotgun. "Anywhere but here."

The field had been dug over fairly recently, and that made running difficult. They stumbled and tripped over furrows, the scent of freshly turned earth filling their nostrils. By the time they reached the other end, both were panting crazily, sweat streaming down backs. Crocker glanced back, only once, and saw the distant farmhouse silhouetted against the darkening sky. A thick column of black smoke belched into the air, while a constant orange flicker played against the empty windows.

"Lewis," Jillian said.

Crocker blinked, but didn't respond.

She nudged him hard in the ribs. "Lewis!"

"What?" he demanded, his temper short fused.

Jillian, hair in disarray, skin paled; neck bruised, dug into her pocket. She pulled out a set of jingling keys. She threw them; Crocker caught them.

"I took them while you and John were arguing in the kitchen," she explained, "They're his Land Rover keys."

"Yeah, but he said the water pump had . . ."

"Rubbish. That Land Rover was his pride and joy. It works just fine, believe me!"

Crocker managed a smile, the shotgun weighing him down.

"Let's move! Billy will be here *any* minute." Jillian said, with a woman's authority.

Off they went.

10

Darkness settled over Oak Ridge.

The streetlamps came on and cast their sodium glare over pavements.

Jillian and Crocker decided that hiding at the inn was a bad idea – Billy Bracket would try there first for certain. Instead, they chose to rest in a cluster of ancient trees that stood near a small park. From here, they sat against an oak's knobbly trunk and drank from a can of Coke, which Crocker had salvaged from the glove box of his battered car.

Leafy boughs and interlaced branches shook and rattled as a breeze sighed through them.

"A shame, really." Jillian muttered, slurping Coke. "I didn't like John, but it's still a shame, isn't it?"

Crocker nodded in the darkness and shifted his position slightly on the damp ground. "I just hope the fire doesn't destroy the Land Rover."

Apparently, the farming vehicle was kept in a barn well away from the main building, but if the wind picked up or hot embers landed on its roof . . .

"When do we make a move?" asked the girl.

"Soon," he whispered, taking the can. "Give it another hour; let the fire burn itself out." He'd tried his mobile again and again, but the reception was gone.

They waited; Jillian dozed. Crocker laid the shotgun across his lap and kept his eyes open and ears alert. Animals scurried past him in the dark. Trees groaned and creaked like arthritic joints. Strange, he thought sleepily, how nobody else, *at all,* had driven through the village all day. Surely that wasn't right. The towns of Bridgnorth and Much Wenlock lay nearby! Yet no other cars had come near.

Crocker's head suddenly snapped up, the heavy blanket of sleep blown apart as he remembered their situation. A noise from dead ahead got his heart galloping.

He blinked and tried to re-gain his night vision. Was that a tall figure inching through the trees towards them? He groped and fumbled with the shotgun, head muddled with sleepy thoughts of home and people he loved. Holy God! It *was* Billy Bracket, the demon himself, creeping and grinning. Crocker noticed with skin- freezing terror that Billy's fingers were all gone. In their place were ten hypodermic needles, all squirting poison like jets of clear urine. Billy Bracket leered and chuckled as he charged towards them, his canine teeth gnashing together.

Crocker screamed like a newborn baby and tried to raise the shotgun to fire, but *my God,* the shotgun was no longer a gun at all! It moved and slithered in his hands, twisted, and bit him.

A snake!

Billy Bracket arrived and plunged both hands down into Crocker's scalp, stabbing him with ten sharp needles that buried themselves deeply inside his throbbing brain.

He screamed and woke up.

His body jerked; heart ready to explode. He recoiled from the shotgun, which, of course, was *just* a shotgun after all, and not a vile black snake.

He whimpered and pressed himself against the tree trunk. There was no Billy Bracket either. Not in here, anyway.

"Wassat?" Jillian mumbled, eyes snapping open.

"Nothing," he breathed, temples aching. He dragged a hand down his face. "Come on; let's get out of this damn village."

They stood up, legs and backs complaining. The night was cooler now, the hour late. Crocker picked up the weapon, gingerly, as if fearing it would buckle and twist in his hands like a squirming serpent. It didn't, all he touched was smooth metal and wood. Jillian took his hand and together they edged past tree trunks and raised roots, ducking beneath thick branches.

"Are you going to kill him?"

He'd been expecting this question all night. "If I have to," he replied, telling the truth. "In self defence, yes, I will."

Before they exited the cluster of trees, Crocker checked both ways, gun barrels thrust out in front of him. Satisfied, they slipped from cover like criminals and hurried over to the main road. It lay in silence, empty of life. Above them, the black sky was strewn with hundreds of stars; scattered diamonds. In other circumstances the sight would have been breath-taking.

They crossed the road at a trot, shoes tapping and scuffing on pavements, like un-trained army cadets on some bizarre mission. The farm was burning itself out; now and again there was the odd flash of fire as it found something new to devour. The house remained upright in the dark though, defiant against torture.

Closer, the air was thick with smoke and reeked of melted plastic.

"What was that name," Jillian whispered as they hurried along. "Baron, something or other! Billy was going on about it days ago, before this shit happened."

"Baron Samedi," Crocker said, half grinning. "Back in Haiti, they believe him to be God of the Graveyard. It's an ancient myth."

"Then why is Billy referring to himself as a myth?" Jillian wanted to know.

Crocker stopped near the farmhouse, and peered right and left. "If you ask me, it's because he's schizophrenic. He should have been incarcerated a long time ago."

She nodded. Whispered a prayer.

Crocker found the Land Rover's keys. Adrenaline surged through his veins.

"He's probably watching us right now," he said, "but we have no choice."

"No."

Crocker dampened his lips and squinted into the gloom. From the burning farmhouse they heard a crash as something collapsed. He held the shotgun tight; it was a reassuring weight in his hands.

He moved off, Jillian following. The bright orange flicker and flash coming from the farmhouse windows cast wobbly shadows across the yard. The hot stench of smoke, scorched brick, plastic and human flesh was enough to make Crocker gag. The yard was strewn with crunchy shards of glass. A good portion of the roof suddenly collapsed inwards, hurling thousands of yellow sparks and embers into the night sky. The noise was deafening, a massive rumbling-roar of wooden struts, tiles and joists. Jillian let loose a startled yelp as something clattered on to the yard at her feet.

Crocker dashed towards the barn where the Land Rover sheltered, heart in his throat. Once at the double-doors he stopped to catch his breath, Jillian right behind him. "Are you okay?" he gasped.

"I think so."

"I'm glad somebody is. I'm scared shitless."

She tittered nervously, and then sobbed.

Propping the shotgun against a fence post, the investigator grabbed the metal door handles and pulled hard. They moved a fraction, but refused to open. He swore and peered closer. A padlock dangled from a hasp. He gave the doors a hard kick.

Jillian was keeping lookout, both of her hands fidgeting. The feeling of being watched was overwhelming, but as yet Billy Bracket and his poisoned goons were keeping a low profile. Yet she sensed eyes in the shadows, she imagined bodies close by, holding knives and other crude weapons, grinning like skeletons, brains turning to slop.

"Hurry up, Lewis," she pleaded.

"It's locked," he told her, nerves tight and twanging. He stared at the Land Rover keys and noticed that there was another, smaller key, hanging off the ring with them. Please God, he thought, please let it fit! I'll be such a good boy, forever and ever amen!

He pushed the smaller key into the padlock's base and gave it a savage twist, and, *Click!* It sprang open. *Thank you, thank you, thank you.*

He tossed the padlock aside, grabbed the handles, and hauled each door open. The air inside the barn was hot and smelt of oil and engine parts. It was dark too, forcing Crocker to dig out his lighter. He ground the flint, raised sparks, which in turn raised his temper, before igniting a slender yellow flame.

There she sat, facing him with her old-fashioned grille and solid metal bumpers.

A throw back from the late 1970s, but nevertheless; she was a sight for sore eyes.

Things are going a little *too* smoothly, he thought, smiling at the Land Rover, which, with its long grille, smiled right back. Almost as if Billy Bracket is *letting* us get this far, before jumping in and crushing all hope.

They could have waited until morning in those trees to give Billy the slip, and walked in to the next town in broad daylight. But Crocker knew that would never happen. If they waited in one place too long, they'd be sniffed out like rats and taken down. No. They needed transport, one that didn't need breaking into and hot-wiring.

He walked over to the driver's side door and, using the cigarette lighter's flame, slotted the correct key into the lock. "Jillian, in here! Hurry up!" he shouted. He swung it open and began to haul himself into the cab.

She entered, carrying the shotgun. Crocker leaned over and shoved open the passenger door; taking the weapon from her shaking hands. She joined him in the cab. He then jammed the ignition key in, closed his eyes, and turned the engine over. It coughed, whined, and then roared into life. The strong diesel engine throbbed beneath the bonnet, eager to go.

He turned on the lights, selected first gear and came off the clutch. The Land Rover pounced forwards and Crocker steered it out of the barn. The headlights illuminating a wooden fence, a field swathed in darkness, and then the gutted farmhouse. He tore his gaze away and floored the gas, gathering speed, heading for the open gate and main road beyond.

"We're going to make it," Jillian said, her hopes soaring.

"If we do, first stop is the police station, and we tell them *everything.*"

"He killed my Mom, Lewis. Of course I'll tell them everything."

Crocker swerved on to the main road, and aimed the Land Rover in the direction of Bridgnorth. As they approached the inn he began to increase his speed, both of them looking at the gloomy building with fearful, tired eyes.

Then it exploded.

The sudden flash momentarily blinded Crocker.

He twisted his face away; eyes squeezed shut. The blast that followed seemed to grab the road surface and flap it like a hearthrug. The Land Rover lost its grip, tyres spinning hopelessly as Crocker slammed on the brakes. He tried to guide the vehicle safely against the kerb but misjudged his speed. It careened off the road and jumped onto the pavement, bounced hard, and smashed into a fence, sending up a shower of broken wood, glass and dirt from the muddy verge.

The night was suddenly floodlit by fire as the inn's windows burst and doors blew off their hinges. The thatched roof ignited, sending up thousands of burning embers and sparks.

A long chunk of drainpipe clattered on to the Land Rover's bonnet and burned merrily, the plastic melting.

Crocker shoved himself back from the steering wheel, his chest throbbing.

He tried to inhale, but that only made the pain worse. "Jillian?" he moaned, glancing over at the passenger seat. She was sprawled across the dashboard, unmoving. *"Jillian!"*

She stirred, said his name under her breath. He sat her back and grabbed at the ignition keys, knowing that the engine had stalled during the crash. Behind them, the inn was a pyre, flames and tumbling smoke. He cranked the engine over, and got a dry whine in reply. "Don't do this," he said, twisting them again. The engine rattled, coughed and died. "No!"

He glanced out of the rear window and knew what he'd see.

Billy Bracket was standing amid burning debris, which was strewn across the road surface like flames peering up from hell. His suit was still immaculate; his smile wicked. He approached the stricken Land Rover almost casually, arms swinging at his sides. Crocker tried to start the engine again, pumping the gas peddle, cursing the lifeless engine with every swear word he knew.

Billy Bracket was almost upon him.

Thinking fast, Crocker lifted his backside off the seat and dragged the meat cleaver from his belt, just as the driver's side door was wrenched open, allowing heat and smoke to pour inside the cab. With those smells came the strong stench of gas.

Billy Bracket's face was a blur through Crocker's watery vision, yet he could make out the grin and hear the words: "We can't be beaten, brother. Do you understand me? Those that were left just laid down their lives to stop you leaving the village. I ask. They obey. It's how I expect things. They blew that building right on cue by rupturing all the gas mains! Now, they are free to wander the next world."

"Suicide," Crocker said huskily. "You made them commit suicide."

"No. They understood. They had to stop you leaving by laying down their lives, man. Yet this is not a problem! With you and the young girl at my side, we will be an all seeing, powerful force. Together we can move on to the next town and gather more people. Perhaps I'll become a new king in your eyes, yes?"

"Kings are men of honour. You're fucking insane."

Billy Bracket's face darkened. He pulled himself up towards the cab, eyes glittering. "If I wanted," he whispered. "I could kill you like I did the farmer. Inject my poison *straight* into your brains! It would be like nothing you've ever felt before."

"I'd rather that," Crocker said angrily, "than become a slave to you!"

The *bokor* grinned, moving his face closer to the investigator's.

"Brother, there is *plenty* where you came from!"

The Voodoo King's breath was hot and rancid, like soured milk.

For a moment Crocker and Billy Bracket locked stares.

Then swiftly, accurately, Crocker swung out with the meat cleaver. It took the *bokor* by surprise, but he was quick enough to let go of the Land Rover's doorframe and bring up his arm in defence. The rusted blade whacked neatly into Billy Bracket's lower arm. It went deep, hacking through his sleeve and flesh alike, coming to rest against his ulna bone. He roared in pain and fell away from the vehicle, dragging the meat cleaver out of Crocker's grasp.

Crocker didn't hesitate. He slammed the door shut and cranked the engine over yet again, a prayer muttered under his breath.

It rattled, clanked, and then, to his disbelief, it boomed into life.

"Lewis?" Jillian said, blinking in confusion, one hand pressed to her forehead.

He ignored the girl and battled the ancient gear stick into reverse. The Land Rover lurched backwards and Crocker steered it on to the main road.

On the muddy grass verge, Billy Bracket yanked the meat cleaver's blade from his lower arm, teeth clenched in agony. The savage wound was gushing blood at a frightening speed, streaming down his fingers and dripping to the ground. He tried to move his hand, but the limb was totally numb and useless.

He saw the blue Land Rover skid to a halt. Heard the gears crunch as the investigator struggled to get it into first. A huge war cry escaped Billy's throat, a howl that would have shamed a werewolf. He ran at the vehicle, meaning to grab one of the doors and simply pull it of its hinges, anything to get at the two people inside! To extinguish their lives with nothing but his bare hands; injured or not.

"Lewis, he's *coming*!" Jillian said in a high, panicky voice.

Crocker shunted and pushed on the stupid gear stick, but it refused to engage first.

He risked a quick glance out of his side window and saw Billy Bracket charging right for them.

He rammed the gear stick forwards, but again he met some infuriating resistance that barred the way. Instead, he thumped it back into reverse and came off the clutch, his right foot planted on the accelerator.

The Land Rover shot backwards just as Billy Bracket reached the door, his good hand attempting to grab the handle. He stepped in to the middle of the road, legs spread, blocking the path should the investigator drive forwards.

Billy Bracket removed one of two remaining hypodermic needles from his jacket pocket. The dosage in this one was meant for one person only.

Himself.

He'd done it before, but only in tiny measures so he wouldn't overdose. Yet this syringe contained the full amount, mixed with a vital shot of adrenaline. Once injected, Billy would know how to use the toxin to his advantage; how to harness the power.

The cure for this toxin hung around his neck on the animal-bone pendant. One of the longer bones was a fluke – hollowed out and filled with salt.

Billy Bracket grinned through his pain and pushed the air from the needle, eyes fixed on the Land Rover.

Crocker hit the brakes, tyres locking on the dry road surface. Smoke billowed thickly from the burning inn, the flicker of fire bright against the dark all around. Billy Bracket stood in the middle of the road, unmoving.

Crocker took in a deep breath. He held it for a moment, and then expelled it from his nostrils. Every part of his weary body ached to go home. His clothes were grimy and torn, his spirits beaten flat.

He watched Billy Bracket lift his good hand, as if to show them something, and then, grinning that wicked grin, he stabbed himself in the wounded arm, the needle going deep into the blooded injury. Pain must have exploded through the entire limb, for the *bokor* threw back his head and shook violently.

Crocker heard Jillian muttering her disgust and horror, but he paid her no heed. Instead, he grabbed the gear stick and thrust it forwards, foot jammed down hard on the clutch. At first it did not accept the change, but he tried again, *forcing* it with gritted teeth. I'm not, he thought, driving out of this village in reverse!

The gearbox let out a wild grating of cogs but, at last, clunked into first.

Billy Bracket tossed the empty syringe aside and began to stride towards the Land Rover, his eyes bulging madly, the whites turning red as blood-vessels haemorrhaged.

The stride turned to a sprint, the sprint to an all-out charge.

"Stop him!" Jillian said, her one hand automatically going for the shotgun. "Lewis, do *something*!"

Crocker death-gripped the steering wheel and watched the voodoo *bokor* running right for them like an enraged bull. He was closing in fast, blood flying from his injured arm.

Crocker let the clutch out and the Land Rover shot forwards to meet him.

Later, these events were smudged and ill defined in Crocker's mind. No matter how hard he tried to remember them with clarity, they remained a blur.

He did remember feeling nothing as the Land Rover jumped into action and sped towards Billy Bracket. He didn't feel a single flicker of emotion as the *bokor* realised he'd made a mistake. He remembered Billy Bracket attempting to leap out of the way, but it was useless. The old metal bumper struck his legs and spun him like a top, shattering a kneecap. He fell sideways and the tyres caught his feet and broke his anklebones; flaying the skin with ease.

Crocker jammed on the brakes and stopped. Billy Bracket rolled three times and lay tangled on the muddy grass verge. He groaned and tried to crawl away, right leg bent at a crazy angle, both feet twisted and pouring blood.

The investigator did not, however, remember putting the Land Rover into reverse, backing off twenty feet, hitting first gear, and roaring towards the grass verge.

Billy Bracket heard the vehicle bearing down upon him. He glanced back over his shoulder, sobbing, eyes dazzled by the headlights. He began to claw at the grass with hooked fingers, pulling his battered body along like a snake. He knew it was pointless, though. Futile. The engine was loud and getting louder. He'd never be able to crawl away in time! He shouted out a curse in his native language and flopped his body over; pain erupting across his legs and broken feet.

The Land Rover came at him and did not stop.

The impact was startling but quick. Billy Bracket saw a brilliant white flare go off behind his eyes, felt a second of burning agony, and then felt nothing more.

The Land Rover sucked the body underneath where it got tangled on the rear axle.

Crocker and Jillian were pitched forwards as the Land Rover jerked to a halt.

Robotically, Lewis Crocker took out his crumpled packet of cigarettes. He removed one and, ignoring the fact it was broken in three places, pushed it between his bloodless lips. It dangled limply, leaking flakes of brown tobacco. Jillian looked at it and snorted, and then, as shock took its toll upon her, began to howl with laughter.

Crocker blinked and frowned, not really understanding. He blinked again and wondered, briefly, why his vision was fogging up. Only when he felt tears dripping from his chin did he realise he was laughing himself.

11

What cut their laughter short was a strange *wobbling* sensation.

At first, Crocker thought he was about to faint, and he quickly shook his head as if to clear it, spitting out the unlit cigarette. Yet Jillian had noticed it too, for her brow creased and she said, "What's that?"

The wobbling became a steady vibration, but not the Land Rover – the *air*. It felt as if the molecules themselves were trembling in fear, causing everything they looked at to blur nonsensically. "I don't . . ." was as far as Crocker got. His voice sounded wet, as if gargling water.

The sudden fission snapped like a mental gunshot. The air split open in front of their eyes – a lightning quick strobe of pure yellow light flooded the interior of the Land Rover. In that brief second Crocker heard noises that made no sense. A keening wail, a deep snarl, so wolfish and hungry, followed by screams that sounded neither male nor female. Then, just as quickly, the fissure in the air closed and the light vanished.

Silence returned. Jillian looked over at Crocker. "What do you suppose *that* was?"

The investigator shook his head, baffled. The mobile phone in his pocket suddenly bleeped. He dug it out and flipped it open. He had full reception.

"Well, well," he said. "Wouldn't you know it?"

Jillian slumped back in her seat, body relaxing. "It's because it's over," she said, with strong conviction. "Billy Bracket *did* cast a spell and you've just broken it!"

"Perhaps. And that light was . . ."

A peek into another dimension?

"Yes?" Jillian wanted to know.

"Forget it. Like you say, it's over."

Over until I go to prison for murder, he thought glumly.

"You were supposed to seduce me, weren't you?" he finally asked.

The question came as a slight surprise to Jillian. Although, at the back of her mind, she knew it would be asked eventually. She nodded.

"Yes, and lure you to Billy's flat. Let him do the rest. I'm sorry," she replied.

"Sick," Crocker said with venom. "Linden Pascal is one sick man!"

"What will you do now?" Jillian said, suddenly feeling very lonely.

Crocker shrugged. "Go to the police, tell them the whole story. I'll even confess what I did to Billy."

"What about Linden?"

Crocker did not reply. He simply opened his door and jumped to the ground.

He's checking Billy's body, Jillian thought with cold disgust. After everything that has happened, he's checking the body for signs of life.

Moments later, Crocker hauled himself back into the cab and slammed the door.

"We should be able to reverse off his body," he said. "He's dead."

They did just that, reversed, steered on to the main road and drove away, heading away from the burning inn, and leaving Oak Ridge behind. For ten minutes they cruised in silence; and in that time – low and behold – they past other cars! Some, if not all, would probably head right through Oak Ridge. Yes, Jillian had been correct. Billy Bracket had used some other form of voodoo to cast a spell over the village, to smother it from the outside world. For those noises he'd heard – the snarling and the screaming as the very air itself healed – had been conformation enough.

As the first lights that announced Bridgnorth came into view, Crocker swung the Land Rover to the kerb and stopped.

"I thought we were going to the police?" Jillian murmured, half asleep.

"Not yet. We will, believe me, but not just yet. I've got to see Linden first."

"Why?"

The investigator's face was set in stern lines of anger. "I've got something for him," he said through clenched teeth. "A little present."

Without further ado, he pulled away and took a right turn, leaving Bridgnorth to slumber in peace.

Jillian wanted to ask what he was doing, but her tired brain was closing down for now, dulling her senses and casting her off into oblivion. She slept soundly.

A little present, Crocker thought as he swept on to the motorway. A grin pulled at his lips as he sped along. *Can't wait to see your face Linden! I really can't.*

Unconsciously, he touched the hypodermic needle in the breast pocket of his shirt. Remarkably, it hadn't been crushed when Billy Bracket's body went beneath the Land Rover. He grinned wider. The look on Linden's face would be hysterical! Wide-eyed; open mouthed and quaking in his Gucci loafers!

Lewis Crocker chuckled to himself, amused by his imaginings.

Seconds later his chuckling turned into loud, body shaking laughter.

At his side, Jillian slept on, unconcerned that she now shared a vehicle with a man who'd finally lost his grip on sanity.

UKUnpublished
.CO.UK

Are you an Author?

Do you want to see your book in print?

Please look at the UKUnpublished website:
www.ukunpublished.co.uk

Let The World Share Your Imagination

Breinigsville, PA USA
11 April 2011
259602BV00003B/8/P

9 781849 440912